# THE Tainted PRINCE

## kiru taye

First Published in Great Britain in 2021 by
**LOVE AFRICA PRESS**
103 Reaver House, 12 East Street, Epsom KT17 1HX
www.loveafricapress.com

ISBN: 978-1-914226-08-3
Also available in ebook format

# ROYAL HOUSE OF SAENE

## THE PRINCESSES:

His Defiant Princess by Nana Prah

His Inherited Princess by Empi Baryeh

His Captive Princess by Kiru Taye

## THE PRINCES:

The Torn Prince by Zee Monodee

The Resolute Prince by Nana Prah

The Tainted Prince by Kiru Taye

The Illegitimate Prince by Empi Baryeh

The Future King by Kiru Taye

# BLURB

Crown Prince Zawadi has prepared for one thing all his life—to become the next king of Bagumi Kingdom. Driven by the need to uphold the traditions and the prestigious name of the Royal House of Saene, he strives to balance culture and technology in building a better nation. Until his perfect world becomes tainted by an assassination attempt and a woman who goes against everything he believes.

To Mr Ahia,

My big brother from another mother.

# PROLOGUE

*MAY 2018*

CROWN PRINCE Zawadi nan Ibrahim Saene's life seemed to be ruled by meetings.

As first-in-line to the throne of the Kingdom of Bagumi, his already immense responsibilities increased after his father, King Ibrahim nan Aziz Saene, had a coronary seizure a year ago.

It seemed more responsibilities equated with more meetings. Meetings with national ministers and lawmakers. Meetings with foreign dignitaries and diplomats. Meetings with family. And on and on it went.

Like the invitation he'd received this afternoon about a conference at his father's reception room, where he was headed this moment.

Private family get-togethers were infrequent and mostly on special occasions these days. His siblings were all adults, living their lives while committed to their duties as serving members of the Royal House of Saene. The active senior royals met every quarter to discuss policy and governance issues concerning the kingdom.

Zawadi saw his father weekly for briefings. Although the king was semi-retired, he liked to be updated on matters of state. That had been one of the caveats to his withdrawal from active duty.

However, this wasn't one of those Friday morning meetings with his father before their trip to the mosque located in the expansive palace grounds. Instead, his assistant had informed him of the impromptu insertion into his schedule only a few hours ago.

Zawadi strode along the endless vaulted corridors of Darusa Palace lit by sunlight through French windows or domed multihued skylights, past stationary uniformed guards and scampering liveried servants. DP, as they fondly referred to the king's stately residence, was made up of sprawling buildings connected by corridors and hidden passages.

He took a shortcut through a sun-drenched interior courtyard, a warm breeze flicking his jacket lapel. Pink bougainvillaea covered a wall, the air scented by roses bushes. That was another noteworthy feature—the magnificent gardens surrounding the buildings.

As he walked through another set of double doors, he spotted his immediate younger brother. Prince Azikiwe, otherwise known as Zik to his siblings, headed towards their father's private quarters.

"What's going on?" Zawadi asked as he levelled up with Zik.

Zik grimaced. "Something came up, and I called an emergency meeting."

So, his brother was the reason for the conference.

"Are Zareb and Zediah joining us?" he asked, stopping briefly outside the doors to the king's private quarters.

"No. This is a sensitive diplomatic issue," Zik replied.

Well, that ruled out the twins, who would rather gouge their eyes out than discuss diplomacy, for different reasons. Zareb was on the 'bludgeon them into submission' end of the spectrum. At the same time, Zediah would rather sit and drink tea with the opponents. As if drinking tea solved the world's problems. Then again, neither was 'hitting the enemy where it hurts' always a viable solution.

Zawadi shook his head in amusement at the thought as the guard announced him and his brother. He stepped into the large reception room first, followed by Zik.

Antique paintings, metal and wooden sculptures documenting the history of Bagumi lined the white walls. A large hand-woven rug covered the aisle from the door to the platform with three hand-carved heavy wooden chairs.

The middle one was embedded with gemstones to signify the grey-haired man's status, who sat on its regal glory. His flowing robe had colourful patterns representing the colours of the gems extracted from the Bagumian mines.

The consorts sat on either side of him—to the right Queen Zulekha, the first wife, and Zawadi's mother. On the left, Queen Sapphire, Zik's mother. They spoke in low tones.

Zawadi and Zik approached the dais and prostrated, a show of submission to their parents. King Ibrahim might be their father, but he was also *the king*.

"Long live King Ibrahim and The Royal House of Saene," they said together.

"Rise, my sons," his father's voice boomed. He leaned forward and pulled Zawadi into a hug first, then Zik.

Zawadi would admit he was not a hugger, but these tactile moments with his parents were priceless. He did the rounds, embracing the two queens as well.

"Mama, is this a new dress?" Zik said. "The fabric is gorgeous."

Zawadi glanced at his brother, who brushed the arm of Queen Zulekha's blue gown.

The senior consort's eyes sparkled as she beamed a smile at his sibling. "Yes, it is. The tailor delivered it yesterday, and I'm wearing it for the first time. Thank you."

"You're welcome, Mama." His brother kissed the queen on the cheek and pulled up a seat beside Queen Sapphire. He met Zawadi's gaze and winked.

Zawadi shook his head as he lowered his body into an armchair, hiding his smile.

He would admit Zik had the charming personality locked down. Zawadi hadn't met any person whom Zik couldn't charm. Especially women. His brother regularly had the queens eating out of his palm. Even the usually shrewd Queen Zulekha seemed to turn into a blushing lady when he turned his attention to her.

One thing he would give his brother. Zik paid attention to things Zawadi would consider trivial. Like noticing the queen's new outfit.

While the dress was lovely, Zawadi hadn't known it was new. It wasn't the kind of detail he would care to note, except when someone else pointed it out.

In any case, if his brother was trying to keep Queen Zulekha sweet, then there must be something grave he wanted to discuss. Which brought them to the reason for the conference.

A servant approached the other side of the bank of chairs and bent to whisper in Zik's ear.

Zik nodded, and the man stepped back towards the side where a projector had been set up.

"Something was brought to my attention that I think you should all see," Zik said. "I won't say any more until you have watched the video. May I play it?"

"Sure. Go ahead," the king confirmed.

Zik turned to the servant and nodded.

The bulbs dimmed, the place lit only by the beam from the projector, which turned the far wall into a giant screen. As this was an internal chamber, there were no exterior windows.

Silence descended into the room. Images rolled across the screen, which Zawadi could only describe as human devastation—demolished buildings, piles of dead bodies, mass graves, refugee camps.

Zawadi's mind went to all the current locations of conflict on the continent.

Was that Darfur, South Sudan? Or the Central African Republic? Perhaps one of the Congos or Angola?

Whatever the location, his stomach hardened, and his chest tightened painfully.

These were Africans. Fellow Africans.

His grief was also tainted by anger. Anger because those in charge of the location obviously did not understand the responsibility of power. Authentic leadership was about the greater good and should never be about personal gain. It wasn't about egos.

Yet, many who wielded power didn't seem to understand or simply didn't care.

From when he'd been a boy, he'd been taught about authority and prepared for leadership. Prepared to rule the Kingdom of Bagumi. That was his duty. He would not fail.

He would be damned if he would fail the citizens of this country by giving into personal whims or something unnecessary.

He accepted that Bagumi and the welfare of its citizens came first about everything else.

But who was going to fight for the aggrieved citizens of the country being shown on screen?

The Royal House of Saene had always intervened where possible during conflicts, especially in West Africa. In the past, they'd sent diplomats, brokered peace deals, and had brought warring factions to the table.

But this didn't exactly look like war. At least there was no mention of combat in the commentary. Instead, the reporter talked about random attacks against unarmed civilians.

Hang on. A name on the bulletin caught his attention. And another one.

Something was wrong.

Zawadi tilted his head and squinted under the flashing light to glare at his brother sitting across the aisle.

As if he expected Zawadi's reaction, Zik stared at him boldly.

What was his brother playing at? Was he trying to ambush Zawadi? For what purpose?

The overhead lamps came on as silence descended when the projection stopped.

Zawadi didn't wait. He couldn't wait.

"Azikiwe, what game are you playing?" Zawadi asked, keeping a tight hold on the annoyance bubbling inside.

"This is no game, brother," his sibling replied in a sombre tone.

"Then the footage must have been doctored ... Fake news."

"I'm afraid not. That is as real as they come. I got it from a reliable source."

Zawadi shook his head. "No. Somebody is trying to stir trouble. You can't trust everything you see. Video-altering software can distort the truth."

"If we can't trust the video, it means we can't trust the Bagumi Intelligence Service."

"What?" Zawadi stared at his brother incredulously.

The consorts gasped, Queen Sapphire's hand flying to her chest.

"Azikiwe, explain yourself," the king ordered, his voice booming with censure.

"Your Majesty," Zik started. "About a month ago, I received credible information about the systematic human rights violations of the people of the Ganuri region of the Wanai Republic. Wanting to verify the news before I could present it to you, I commissioned the Bagumi Intelligence Service to investigate the validity of the allegations."

Zik had ties to the BIS, the covert operations responsible for investigating organised crime, extremist and terrorist organisations, and threats to national security. He'd completed the mandatory national service with them after his post-graduate studies.

"On whose authority?" the king asked the question at the tip of Zawadi's tongue.

His brother could have triggered an international crisis with their regional neighbour by sending spies into Wanai. There could still be repercussions from the video alone.

"Mine, Your Majesty. I thought it was best to keep you and Zawadi out of the loop lest something went wrong. Therefore, you would have plausible deniability, and your integrity would not be compromised. And I would take the blame alone."

Okay. Zik had thought it through and had been willing to bear the consequences.

Still, Zawadi asked, "And when did you get the video?"

"The intelligence officers returned last week. I met them and watched the footage."

This was getting worse.

"Hang on. You've been sitting on this information for a week?"

What excuse would his brother produce this time?

"I had to travel to Wanai the day after I watched the video. As you were aware, our sister, Isha, was visiting her fiancé, Kweku, at the time. Due to the circumstances, her immediate safety was important, and I had to extract her securely. Once we returned, other matters grabbed my attention. Consequently, this was the earliest opportunity to discuss it with the rest of you."

Zik made a vital omission.

Isha's ex-lover had abducted her. Her old university lecturer had snatched her from a hotel in Nigeria and taken her to Wanai. Kweku had rescued her from the terrorist. He'd taken her to the presidential palace in Wanai, where Zik had picked her and brought her home.

However, they hadn't informed their father about the abduction. So Zawadi would not mention it now. He didn't need to aggravate the old man or trigger another heart attack since Isha was now home and safe.

A palace guard approached and spoke to Zik in a low voice.

"Excuse me for a moment," Zik said before following the man out of the door.

"Do you really think the footage is fake?" Queen Zulekha asked in a severe tone.

"I don't know," Zawadi replied honestly. "Our intelligence service would not create fake videos. For what purpose?"

"No." His mother wore a pensive expression. "Our intelligence service would not stoop to such levels. They know it would be easy to test the video for veracity. And the culprit would pay a heavy price."

"Which leaves a troubling reality," the king chimed in. "Our allies have not been frank with us. According to that report, Kweku Doona is responsible for many of the atrocities."

"I'm shocked, Your Majesty. Pardon me for not rushing to condemn him until I can double-check the evidence."

He needed undeniable, irrefutable evidence before he would vilify a man he'd called his friend for over fifteen years.

He'd known Kweku Doona since they were at the military academy as teenagers. As first sons of heads of states, they'd become fast friends and had been on adventures together.

In recent times, they'd accepted significant governance roles and challenging obligations, which meant they didn't see each other often anymore. Nevertheless, they communicated by phone and other messaging services regularly.

About a year ago, Kweku and Isha got engaged.

Zawadi looked forward to cementing his friendship with Kweku by becoming his brother-in-law.

Talk about the devil.

The far door opened, and Isha entered the reception room hand in hand with a man.

Zawadi's body stiffened. He ground his teeth as recognition dawned.

Professor Bassong? How did the man get into the palace? Where the hell was Zareb? Did he know about this?

As Isha greeted their parents, Mr Bassong stood in the aisle.

Zawadi glared at the man, hands balled by his sides.

He wanted to punish the professor for what he did to Isha when she was a young student. Hell, he should lock the man up and throw away the key.

Imagine a lecturer seducing his student. That's what the man had done to Isha. She hadn't even been out of her teen years when the two had met. Mr Bassong was ten years older and had been the lecturer in a position of power. He had abused that power by preying on Isha, seducing her, and then abandoning her.

Such immoral men shouldn't be allowed to walk around freely.

Now, here he was in the palace, apparently with Isha's consent. What did Isha see in such a person? Didn't she realise the professor probably did the same things to other women?

Worse, the man had become the leader of a terrorist organisation.

If Zawadi was a gambling man, he would bet that all the atrocities they'd just viewed on the video were due to Mr Bassong and his militia, the MLG.

Isha turned to Zawadi and greeted him.

"I was not aware that you had a guest." Zawadi didn't hide his displeasure at seeing her former lecturer in their midst.

Isha seemed to take it as her cue to introduce the professor, who in turn prostrated before the king.

Zawadi jerked back in surprise. He hadn't been expecting the gesture from the guest. His friend, Kweku, had never prostrated, choosing only to bow before the king.

It seemed the visitor was here on a charm offensive. Hopefully, the king would see through the act.

But things went in a different direction, and the king gave the man an audience, allowing him to state his case with Isha reminding everyone about the situation in Ganuri.

"Oh, yes," Queen Sapphire said. "Those were horrible scenes. Imagine all those women and children in those camps. We must do something about it."

"We are, Mum," Isha said. "We've submitted a case file to the International Criminal Courts who have started their investigations."

"Does Kweku know about this?" Zawadi asked, unable to contain the contempt from his siblings. They had bypassed him, bypassed protocol, and already filed a case with the ICC. Azikiwe and Isha had pulled some stunts in the past. But this was the worst. How dare they?

"Yes, he does. He and his father are the accused."

Zawadi had heard enough of the nonsense. "You can't be serious. The only person guilty of a crime is the terrorist you brought into this palace." He pointed at Mr Bassong. "Papa, that man is the lecturer Isha had an affair with when she was in London. He is also the leader of the separatist group fighting to split from Wanai."

"No, it's not true. He's not a terrorist." Isha stepped down to stand beside the professor.

Of course, his sister would deny it. Like she hadn't been cohabiting with the man for the past month when she should've been preparing for her wedding to Kweku.

Mr Bassong took Isha's hand. Right there in front of everyone.

Zawadi loved his sister. *But Almighty give him strength.* Did she not have any shame? How could she have rekindled her doomed love affair with the professor only weeks to her wedding?

There were certain behaviours not allowed in the presence of the king. No public displays. Holding hands with a man to whom she wasn't engaged being one of them.

Why couldn't Isha obey simple rules?

Zawadi quashed the urge to walk down the dais and separate the two.

Then the guest pleaded for the king's forgiveness about his previous illicit affair with Isha and asked for their father's permission to marry her now.

What effrontery. The man had *cajones* after what he'd done.

"That may be so, young man," the king said. "But no terrorist is going to marry my daughter."

Thank goodness their father wasn't easily swayed by talk.

"Your Majesty," Mr Bassong said. "I swear to you, on my life, that I've never committed any of the crimes Kweku Doona accuses me of. Prince Azikiwe sent spies into Ganuri to document the events. Suppose he found any evidence of members of my group persecuting the citizens. In that case, I'm sure he would have presented them to you today."

"That's true, Papa." Zik joined Isha and Mr Bassong on the aisle. "The intelligence officers that went into Ganuri found no evidence of crimes committed by the MLG. Instead, the group have provided safe zones and shelter for the people who've been attacked. Nevertheless, there is a genocide going on, and all fingers point to Doona, especially Kweku who has been arresting and torturing the people campaigning for independence."

The hits kept coming. Now, Zik was blaming Kweku for the atrocities? What was wrong with his siblings? Kweku was no angel, but this was farfetched.

Soon the proceedings flew away from him, regardless.

Their father proclaimed that there would be a wedding between Isha and Mr Bassong, and everyone stood to congratulate the new couple.

Zawadi stood still, reeling from the shock, when Zik came up to him and patted his shoulder. "Don't take this personal. You should know Isha well enough. When she wants something, she will move Heaven and Hell to make it happen."

Yes, Isha's determination and ability to make things happen were well documented around here. Still, it wasn't his sister's stubbornness filling him with concern.

"But how can you accept him so readily after what he did to her?" Zawadi tilted his head in Mr Bassong's direction.

Zik shrugged. "I accept him because I know how much Isha loves him."

"Even if he's not good enough for her?" Zawadi just couldn't comprehend such a fanciful notion. Romantic love wasn't something he thought about, nor had he ever experienced it.

"Grandma used to say that true love is unconditional. The heart yearns for whom it yearns." Zik wore a forlorn expression Zawadi had never seen before for a few seconds. Then he shook his head, wiping the face. "Maybe one day you'll understand the idiom."

Zawadi nearly laughed. He would never be too besotted and become unable to tell right from wrong. He didn't have his head in the clouds.

There was already a woman in his life. Soon they would be married and live happily ever after, just like his parents.

# CHAPTER ONE

*February 2019*

Zawadi sat on a plush leather sofa in the games room, sipping the fruit-infused ice water. He half-listened to his brothers bantering while he caught up with personal messages.

Nathan, his assistant, screened his professional memos. But Zawadi liked to maintain his personal contacts.

A few years ago, Azikiwe redesigned the disused music room in the Sahel wing of Darusa Palace into a masterfully outfitted arcade or mancave as they jokingly referred to it.

Soundproofed, with fantastic acoustics, the walls were black. The surfaces were sleek and shiny, with marble flooring and ample lighting. It was all sophisticated fixtures and cabinetry.

From the futuristic comforts of plush leather sofas and the remote-controlled cosy recliners to state-of-the-art technology and the newest consoles, which took gaming into a sleek transcendentally experience. There were massive HD screens and top-notch sound systems.

They even had a fitted bar with classy stools and a granite counter. The place turned into a party zone when they had friends visiting. There was even a mini casino along with the billiards and foosball tables. Next door was a fully functional theatre which they used for screening international movies before they were available at public cinemas.

"I can't believe you brought a woman in here, of all things." Zareb sat on another sofa, facing an HD screen. In his hand was a controller for one of the games consoles.

"Of all things? A woman isn't things." Zik sat next to him, holding a second controller. On the massive display, digital sports cars raced against each other on a virtual track. Zik was obsessed with race cars. In another life, he could've become a Formula One race driver. But being a royal prince came with restrictions. Driving fast cars for a living was out of the question.

"Well, you know what I mean. This is supposed to be a bachelor pad, a *man* cave. No women allowed. That's the rule." Zareb said.

"Well, technically, the rule is that no woman is allowed in here when there are two or more of us gathered," Zik said. "I brought Tosini here when no one else was here. She wanted to see the man cave, and I obliged her."

He shrugged nonchalantly.

"But I walked in on the two of you. I swear I'm never playing billiards again."

"Stop being a baby. Okay. I'll have the tabletop re-laid. Or better still, I can scrap the whole thing. We can even put the table up for auction for one of the queens' charities.

"And give the two queens coronaries when they find out the table's soiled history."

Zawadi couldn't help shaking his head as the men laughed aloud. "No. You will not donate the table to a charity auction."

He had no doubt the value would go up if his brother's antics were revealed. But he would never intentionally approve any activity that would sully the reputation of the Royal House.

"Where is Zed, by the way? He's supposed to be here this evening," Zawadi said.

They'd played a game of rugby earlier in the sports field at the edge of the extensive palace grounds. Every quarter there was a princes-vs-guards Rugby Sevens match, which they took very seriously. The princes didn't like to lose to their guards. Today had been one of the weekly practice sessions.

The core team comprised Zawadi, Zik, Zareb, Ejike Onoh, Ekene Onoh, Osei Asante, and Razi Hamadou. They made time in their busy schedules and showed up regularly for training.

Osei was an Asante prince and a distant relative of Razi who wasn't a royal. However, Razi was Zik's friend. The two had worked briefly together while Zik had been undertaking his national service. In addition, Razi's brother, Kojo, was Isha's personal bodyguard and played rugby for The Royal Guards.

The Onoh brothers were Igbo princes and family friends. Their oldest brother, Osita, used to participate but only showed up for significant events these days.

Others filled in as substitutes and made up the twelve-man squad for match days.

"Is everything okay with Zed," Zik asked. "He's been looking a bit forlorn lately."

"You mean more than usual," Zareb quipped.

"Don't be like that." Zik shook his head.

"Alright. All right. I'll find out what's keeping him." Zareb removed his headset and dropped the controller.

When he disappeared through the door, Zawadi spoke. "I want to talk to you before the twins return."

Zawadi rose from his seat, walked over, and settled on the sofa next to Zik.

"Okay. What's up?" Zik asked, restarting the game.

"I need your help." Zawadi grabbed the controller to set himself up. He wasn't a gamer per se but liked to participate occasionally.

Zik glanced around the room as if expecting someone else to be there. "Come again."

"I said I need your help." His fingers tapped the buttons, sending his virtual car hurtling along the track on screen.

"Me? You want my help?"

"Why do you sound so surprised?"

"Because you've never asked for my help before. I'm charm and chaos. You're calm and composure. We operate on different ends of the spectrum. How could I possibly help you?"

Zawadi sighed. His brother was right. They were different people. More to the point, Zawadi didn't usually ask for help. Instead, whatever he commanded was executed by others. He'd never felt the need to seek support because it had always been given one way or the other.

Nonetheless, he found himself in a difficult situation.

Nine months ago, the king gave his consent for Isha to wed Professor Bassong. Afterwards, Zawadi re-evaluated his relationships with those around him, especially his siblings.

Introspection wasn't the most natural thing for him. He'd been raised to focus on others—his duty to the country and the people's welfare—not on himself. He maintained his physical health because he'd been trained to do so, and it had become a habit. However, examining his emotional or mental processes was alien.

Still, the incident between Isha and Kweku nine months ago had caused him to do some soul-searching. He hadn't liked what he'd found out about himself.

For the first time in his adult life, he needed help with the matter bothering him.

The two royal families—Saene and Onoh—had agreed many years ago to strengthen and formalise their friendship through the marriage between the Bagumian crown prince and the Onoh princess.

Zawadi and Amara were bound to fulfil their parents' pact because Amara was the only Onoh daughter and Zawadi was the Bagumian crown prince.

"You know I recently had a conversation with Mama about getting married," he spoke. "Since our sisters got married, Papa is concerned that his plans to secure the future of the kingdom and our lineage may go awry. So, the families have set a date for the Igbankwu traditional ceremony to formalise my marriage contract with Amara Onoh."

Zik's body stiffened. The car on his screen went off the road and smashed into a wall. He mouthed a low curse. Yanked the headphones off his head and tossed everything on the low glass table.

"Are you okay?" Zawadi asked as sudden coldness hit his core. He'd never seen his brother lose control of the game in this manner.

"I need a drink." Zik straightened and headed for the bar.

"Is it wise at this hour?" Zawadi asked before he could sanction himself.

He was teetotal by choice. But some of his siblings consumed alcohol. He never tried to lecture them. They were adults.

Still, Zik reaching for a drink right now when they'd all been drinking non-alcoholic beverages after the sports practice felt wrong.

"Wise? No. But I don't care. All this talk about marriage gives me the heebie-jeebies. If I want to get sloshed, I will." He grabbed the whiskey decanter and poured into a short, cuboid, crystal tumbler. He raised the glass in a silent toast, tossed his head back and drank. When he lowered it, he said, "Well, you said you needed my help?"

Zawadi eyed his brother.

A pulse ticked on Zik's temple, his jaw was tight, and his gaze fixed straight ahead. He was usually carefree, a little too carefree for Zawadi's liking sometimes and had never expressed irritation in this manner before.

Zawadi should probe Zik to discover what had upset him. He didn't buy the flippant comment about marriage heebie-jeebies. However, the twins would show up any minute, making their private time short. So, he would bring it up later.

"I need your help to find Kweku Doona," he blurted out.

Zik's brows squished together in apparent confusion. "You need my help to find Kweku. He's your friend. Can't you find him yourself?"

Good question.

Zawadi grimaced and cleared his throat. "When the atrocities in Wanai became international news, I couldn't very well maintain direct contact with him. Then he went into hiding in exile after the coup, and we lost touch completely. After what Isha told me about him, my mind has been unsettled. I think he should stand in a court of law to answer for his crimes."

"Does Isha know about this?" Zik asked, sitting up and facing him, seemingly more interested.

"Not really. You know she and the professor have their hands full in Wanai with a looming election. I want to talk to Kweku directly, one-on-one. I need explanations for his actions."

"Well, I'm sure if you contact the Bagumi Intelligence Service, they will undertake the assignment."

"I know. But this needs to be off the records. I need to go through unofficial channels, which is why I need you to do it. The same way you got them to send spies into Wanai."

"So, you, Mr Rules and Regulations, wants me to break the rules and send spies to find Kweku Doona?"

"Yes."

"And what do they do once they've found him?"

"I want him lured to a location where I can talk to him man-to-man."

"Okay. Consider it done."

Before Zawadi could thank him, the twins walked in, heading toward the bar.

"Are we telling them?" Zik asked in a low voice.

"Telling us what?" Zareb asked, looking from Zik to Zawadi. The man had an acute hearing. "What did I miss?"

"I asked Zik to find Kweku Doona," Zawadi said simply. But there was nothing simple about his words. He was going against protocol, and his brother would pull him up on it.

"Find Kweku?" Zareb still looked confused.

"Off the records. No one can know that I commissioned the investigation," Zawadi clarified.

"Damn," Zediah commented, reflecting the gravity of the situation. He climbed onto one of the stools next to Zik.

"You're going to need this." Zik lifted another glass of whiskey he'd just poured.

Zareb snatched the drink and downed a gulp. He slammed the glass on the counter. "This is not a good idea. You are the crown prince. You cannot be seen or even have it implied that you are enquiring about Kweku Doona until he has been apprehended and had his day in court."

Zawadi rubbed his knuckle along the bridge of his nose. "That's why Zik is doing it on my behalf."

"When the shit hits the fan, I'll be the one carrying the blame." Zik took another sip of his drink.

Zawadi winced, skin heating. He was putting his brother in a difficult situation. But there was no other option. If he went through the proper channels, he would be shut down before the project took off. Zik was used to circumnavigating the rules. No one would bat an eyelid where he was concerned because he didn't have as much at stake as Zawadi.

"Finding Kweku is important. He should pay for what he did to all those people. For what he did to our sister," Zediah said.

"I know." Zik sighed.

"And I wouldn't ask you to do it if I had another option," Zawadi said.

"I know. Don't mind me. I'm just a little wound up this evening." Zik commented.

"What is it? PMS?" Zareb said and laughed at his own joke. The others just shook their heads while smirking. "Okay. I know when I'm outnumbered. So, let it be on the record that I warned you against this course of action. But it's all for one and one for all. So, let's do it."

"All for one," they cheered, clinking glasses. When they were younger, they used to refer to themselves as The Musketeers. Well, The Three Musketeers and D'Artagnan. Zareb was D'Artagnan because he was the youngest and the cockiest.

Zediah stepped off the stool, headed across the room and picked up the cue stick. "Who fancies a billiards game?"

"I wouldn't touch that if I were you," Zareb said. "You don't know where it's been."

The siblings burst into laughter at the confused expression on Zediah's face.

# CHAPTER TWO

*July 2019*

Danai Ruga navigated around the partygoers, her gaze sweeping the spacious ballroom.

Finally, she spotted the target, a dark-skinned man in a half-undone maroon silk shirt and a gold-chained medallion glittering against his oiled chest. He lounged on a sofa, slacks-clad legs spread wide, arms draped on women in skimpy clothes. His table was covered with bottles and flutes of champagne.

For a man who was supposed to be in exile, Kweku Doona wasn't doing much hiding within the city he'd spent the last few weeks. The son of the former president of Wanai, he was accused of atrocities, including mass murder and ethnic cleansing. His father was currently under house arrest awaiting trial, and Kweku had slipped out of the country with other members of his family.

Danai had been part of the team from Bagumi sent into Wanai to gather evidence about the crimes against humanity. Appalled by what she'd seen happening to fellow Africans, she'd wanted to go hunt the Doonas herself.

Three months ago, her boss, Razi Hamadou, informed her of a new op to 'search and grab' Mr Doona. So here she was.

"I've got eyes on Dingo," she said for the tiny microphone, which looked like a button attached to her dress.

Dingo was the code name they used for the target, Kweku.

Her colleague, Vaugh, attired in a black tuxedo, stood at the edge of the sleek bar. He glanced at her and gave an almost imperceptible nod.

Danai only saw it because she stared at him, and they'd worked together long enough to pick up body language others would miss.

This was her cue to move in.

Danai sashayed towards Kweku. Her athletic figure was wrapped in a knee-length body-hugging black dress. It was stretchy enough to allow freedom of motion when she needed to move fast. With minimal makeup on her face—lip gloss and mascara—her natural hair was in neat cornrows beneath the tresses of front-lace weave wrapped into an elegant bun at her nape.

She ignored the pain from the three-inch stilettos pinching her feet.

It couldn't be helped, though.

In her relaxed state, she lived in tank tops and jeans, wore overalls while getting greasy under damaged cars at her dad's mechanic shop or strapped on leathers when she rode her bike.

But tonight, she had to be glammed up and dressed to impress like all the other people at the party. Or for her, dressed to attract one person. She'd worn similar clothing to what the target liked in his women. She had studied his dossier and learned everything about him to help her accomplish her mission.

Tonight was about work. So uncomfortable shoes came with the territory as an undercover agent.

The women wore cocktail dresses, and the men wore suits. The event was invitation only. She'd only wangled an invitation through Prince Azikiwe Saene of the Bagumi Kingdom.

Prince Zik, as he was fondly known, the second son of the Bagumian king, was a famous flirt. There weren't any A-list parties within Africa, the Middle East or even Europe that he wasn't invited.

He was supposed to attend this event. But they didn't want to spook the target who would recognise Prince Zik on sight. So Danai and her team were here instead.

Security was tight because of the star-filled guest list. She had already spotted famous actors, top musicians and people who frequently hit the richest Africans lists. Bling made the venue sparkle. Women with gemstones-encrusted earrings and necklaces, men sporting expensive glittering wristwatches and cufflinks made from the most precious metals.

Blending in was Danai's thing. Due to her job, she met celebrities she wouldn't have interacted with in her private life and witnessed them in all kinds of conditions.

When she'd been a child, she'd dreamt about being a secret agent, travelling the world on different adventures on His Majesty's Secret Service.

As an adult, she lived the dream, although it wasn't always as glamourous as this. Last year's trip to the Ganuri region of Wanai was a prime example of some of the horrors encountered on the job.

Also, unlike the fictional James Bond character, she didn't get to introduce herself as Ruga, Danai Ruga. The whole point of being a secret agent was to acquire a new persona with each mission to prevent her identity from being discovered. So, she rarely used the same name more than once.

Now, she settled on the bank of leather sofas directly in front of Kweku's section so he could get a view of her. She kept the cocktail tumbler in her hand that she had ordered at the bar. It was more of a prop than anything. She didn't like to drink on the job except where it presented the image she wanted to show off.

A couple of men approached Danai, and she dismissed them as politely as possible with a lie— she was here with her fiancé. He was in conference with one of the other guests.

"Cam, how is it going?" Razi's voice sounded in her head, from the tiny earpiece hidden by the tresses of hair.

Cam was the nickname her teammates had given her. It was short for Chameleon because of her ability to change her appearance fluidly. She had one of those faces that could be boyish without makeup, albeit a pretty one due to the high cheekbones. Yet a dash of lipstick and mascara, and she was all female.

Danai lifted the glass to cover her mouth, pretending to drink as she spoke. "He's noticed me but is yet to make a move."

From what she'd read about him, Kweku was one of those men who thought they were God's gift to women. He was known to impose himself on women, primarily single, available ones like she was posing. Of course, Kweku already had women hanging around him. But apparently, that had never stopped him before.

"Maybe I should've been the one in a pretty dress, strutting my stuff," Vaugh said on the earpiece, his voice filled with amusement.

Danai tried not to spew the tiny sip of scotch and ginger ale all over her outfit.

Vaugh was built like a brick house, and the image of him in a form-fitting dress and high-heels made Danai nearly burst into giggles. Likewise, there was laughter on the line from Razi. She got on brilliantly with the members of the team. They treated her like one of the lads, which worked fine for her. So, nothing was off-limits for their banter, even when they were working on a tense operation.

Before she could respond with a witty remark about what she thought about Vaugh in a dress, a server in a black-on-black uniform approached.

"Excuse me, ma'am," he said.

"Yes." She lifted her gaze to the man, her expression blank. "How can I help you?"

"The gentleman over there—" he indicated the target with his finger "—will like to invite you to join him."

It seemed Mr Doona was on form tonight.

Danai smiled as she glanced in his direction. He lifted his drink while giving her a smirk.

Danai returned her gaze to the waiter. "I don't know the gentleman. Who is he?"

"That is Mr Charles Mensah," the waiter replied.

Kweku's new assumed name. He could hardly introduce himself as Kweku Doona when the man with that name was on an international wanted list. Yet, here with a fake name, no one was batting an eyelid.

Not her, though. Not the Bagumi Kingdom. She was proud to be Bagumian, considering they were unwilling to play blind, deaf and dumb where the Doonas were concerned.

"Please tell Mr Mensah that if he wants to talk to me, he will have to come over here," Danai said, leaning into her seat and sipping her drink.

Rumour had it Kweku liked his women to play hard-to-get. He wanted to prove he could get any women, even the difficult ones.

The server walked to the other side of the lounge and leaned over to speak to Mr Doona.

Kweku patted the thighs of the women sitting on both sides of him and stood.

"Target is in motion, heading to Cam," Vaugh spoke so that all the members of the team could listen as Danai watched Kweku walk towards her.

He sat down beside her without an invitation.

"I didn't invite you to sit," Danai said, feigning annoyance.

"Yes, you did," his voice sounded slurry. If he was already drunk, then the mission might go a lot more smoothly. "You told me to come over here if I wanted to speak to you. So here I am."

"Fair enough." Danai nodded, keeping up the disinterested charade. "What did you want to speak to me about?"

"I want to get to know you. This is a party, after all, and you seemed lonely all by yourself." He grinned, teeth bared like a shark's. "What's your name?"

"My name is Cameron."

"Cameron? Isn't that a boy's name?"

"No. It's actually unisex. You should know there's a famous actress with the same name."

"Of course. I must have forgotten that. Let me get you a drink."

"No. Let me get you a drink. What are you having?"

"Champagne, of course."

"Of course." She smiled and got up.

All worked well since the champagne bubble would hide the fizz of the tranquiliser.

A stroll to the bar, and she met Vaugh, who handed her the already doctored champagne glass with another glass of Scotch mixer. Since he could hear the conversation on the transmitter, he knew what to order before she arrived at the bar. She returned to the sofa and settled next to Kweku.

As expected, he started pawing her skin. She didn't bother to resist.

"How about we go back to my place for a private party?" he said, looking worse for wear.

"Sounds like a good idea. How far is your place?" Danai asked.

"Not far. I'm staying in a villa by the beach."

"Great. Let's have a private party," she whispered against his ear, cupping the bulge in his trousers.

He grinned and tried standing but wobbled.

Shit. The drug seemed to be taking effect already. She needed to get him out of here.

She wrapped her arms around his waist, taking some of his weight and guided him towards the hotel exit. The attendant held the doors, and they stepped into the warm night air. The sea breeze flapped leaves in the trees.

"My car." Kweku reached in his pocket and withdrew a card for the valet who went to bring the car around.

"You are in no state to drive," she said.

"I'm perfectly okay."

But as the car stopped in front of them, he swayed. No way would she let him drive.

"Help me get him into the passenger seat," she said to the valet.

The man guided Kweku to the other side and strapped him in while Danai got into the driver's seat of the Ferrari and reset the seating. She tipped the valet and gunned the engine, driving out of the extensive ground and through the security checkpoint.

Once she was on the main road, she didn't head towards Kweku's residence, one of the expensive beachside homes. Instead, she headed towards the cliffs.

"Package secured," she said for the benefit of her team listening to the transmitter.

"Great." The response came from Razi. "Meet us at the rendezvous point."

Kweku stirred in his seat. "Who are you talking to?"

"Just to the voices whispering in my head," she said with amusement.

Another glance at Kweku showed he had passed out.

About thirty minutes later, she stopped at a layby on the road, leading to one of the beaches. The road wound around the mountain and had sheer cliff faces. A grey van was already parked there.

Danai pulled up beside it and got out. Razi and Vaugh got out of the van and dragged Kweku out and into the back of the truck. They bound him with ropes.

Meanwhile, Danai stuck a rag into the tank of the Ferrari. She lit the edge of the rag as Razi and Vaugh pushed the car. Then, as it tumbled down the cliff already ablaze, they all got into the van and drove away.

Razi drove them toward the docks, where they would board a boat headed out of the country. Luckily, the ports were only a few minutes away. They had chosen a rendezvous point that would not cause significant delays once they had set the car on fire. The burning car would attract attention on a dark night.

"It seems like such a shame to destroy a perfect Ferrari," Vaugh commented when they pulled into the enclosed warehouse they had hired.

"It's more of a shame that the Doona bastard was not in it when we shoved it down the cliff," Danai said.

"Good point. But we are not the judge or jury here. Otherwise, we're no different from him."

Danai knew that quite well. She just hoped this time, the people who deserved justice after what Kweku Doona had done to them would get it.

# CHAPTER THREE

The speedboat cut across the Atlantic Ocean in a straight line lit by navigation lights, although a half-moon sat in the cloudless night sky. Land was about thirty minutes behind them.

Danai didn't recognise the man at the helm piloting them to their destination. He'd met them at the harbour. She and Razi had boarded with the still unconscious Kweku while Vaugh had stayed on land. He would be there to pick them when they returned.

Their destination loomed in the distance. A yacht moored in the middle of the ocean lit up like the Las Vegas strip. Two smaller patrol boats circled the luxury yacht.

Did this monstrosity belong to Prince Zik?

He'd been the one who commissioned their assignment, and the instruction was to deliver Mr Doona to this location.

Danai's mouth dropped open as the speedboat pulled up alongside. More men appeared and lifted Kweku up to the yacht. He would no longer be their problem.

Instead of steering the speedboat around, the man at the helm spoke. "His Royal Highness would like a word with both of you."

"Okay?" Razi glanced at Danai.

"Sure." She shrugged. Not like she was in a hurry to be anywhere else. Or had much choice about refusing the prince's summons.

She'd met Prince Zik once before. He was one of the most laidback people she'd ever met, considering he was a member of the esteemed and noble Royal House.

Razi led the way as they climbed onto the yacht.

"Welcome, aboard. I'm Nathan, Assistant to His Royal Highness." a man in a dark suit and tie greeted. He was not as tall as Danai, yet his chest was puffed out, and his chin raised in a self-important manner.

"Thank you. I'm Razi Hamadou, and this is my colleague, Danai Ruga."

"It's nice to meet you," Danai said as they shook hands.

"This way, please." The man swivelled and walked along the right side of the deck—starboard—towards the front of the boat—the bow—if she recalled the correct sailing terms.

"How big is this thing?" Danai muttered. She had to pick her mouth off the floor when they rounded the corner to the bow.

A helicopter stood on the deck. There was a freaking helicopter pad on the yacht!

Okay. She knew these princes were loaded. But this?

Bagumi was one of the stable economies in Africa. It had a small population compared to the giants like South Africa and Nigeria. The rare metals and gems from their mines ensured a healthy economy, which guaranteed free education for every child up to the tertiary level. The average person lived above the poverty line.

Yet, she couldn't accept such excesses even for a playboy prince like Azikiwe.

Disappointment gnawed at her gut because she had pegged him as down-to-earth and not as snobbish as his siblings. Went to show that everyone had a vice.

The heels of her shoes tapped against the hard flooring. A reminder she was still dressed in the stunning outfit and looking like a guest on the yacht.

They descended below deck before Nathan opened a door, bowed, and announced them. "Your Royal Highness, presenting Mr Hamadou and Ms Ruga."

He stepped out of the way.

The formal introductions confused Danai for a second. She hadn't been introduced in the same manner when she'd first met the king's second son months ago. So why was it required now? Anyway, Prince Zik and Razi were friends, weren't they? She'd picked up the vibes from the said first meeting. So why the need for formality?

Danai followed Razi into a spacious living room decorated in varying earth tones of leather sofas with contrasting cushions and polished wood flooring. The rows of bright overhead spotlights and shiny, spotless surfaces made her blink several times.

Years of training and experience as an undercover agent taught her to mask her emotions.

This became handy now as she stifled a gasp as her body tensed.

It wasn't the easy-going, charming Prince Zik in the room.

It was his older brother.

Crown Prince Zawadi Saene of the Kingdom of Bagumi sat on one of the sofas as if it were a throne and him a king. She had never met him before. But there would be no adult in Bagumi who wouldn't be able to recognise the man as he had been raised in the public gaze from infancy as the next in line to the throne.

The man was known to be brilliant and driven. He was stunning and imposing, even seated. Tall and broad-shouldered, his features were handsome and strong.

His expression made her breathless. He watched her with curiosity. Fascination.

She wasn't usually starstruck, as was proven tonight at the Cape Verdean hotel, which had been full of the rich and famous. She was always cool and calm under pressure. Yet as she stepped into the room and stared at the royal prince, the man who would become the next ruler of her country, she was suddenly self-conscious as his dark gaze settled on her.

Her skin flushed with heat under his piercing gaze. She wished she had changed into regular clothes or at least was wearing trousers and a shirt. Not this expensive couture gown and stilettos which made her look and, weirdly, feel delicate under his scrutiny.

She was used to not being noticed and being able to blend in the background. Hence she'd earned the nickname Chameleon.

Yet the prince's unwavering gaze rested on her face intently in a way no one had done before. Her skin prickled, heat washing through her. Her mouth dried out, and her heart raced. She should have waited out on the boat or even in the van instead of Vaugh.

Her knees wobbled, and she cursed her high heels as warmth unfurled in her belly.

"Your Highness." Razi dipped his head and nudged Danai with his elbow.

Danai recovered her composure and curtsied, her cheeks heated. "Your Highness."

"Welcome. Sit." His voice was deep, smooth, and seductive.

Goosebumps skittered over her bare arms as if he was addressing only her and there was no one else in the room.

She lifted her head and moved to sit on one of the sofas beside her colleague.

"Razi, it's good to see you," the prince said. "We haven't seen you at the rugby training in recent weeks."

Why was the prince talking in such a familiar tone?

"It's good to see you too, Your Highness," Razi replied, reminding Danai he would be acquainted with the crown prince since he was friends with Prince Zik. "Work has kept me away from Bagumi recently. But I am looking forward to training with you all again soon."

"That's good. We need you back in the scrum-half position for the next tournament."

"Of course." Razi grinned.

The prince paused and met Danai's gaze, demanding her full attention. His clear, steady stare made her think of the great kings of Bagumi and especially his father, King Ibrahim. He looked like his forebear.

Damn. He was ridiculously handsome. Pictures of him online or in newspapers didn't do him justice. If he smiled, he would give his charming immediate brother a run for his money.

From what she'd read about him, he must be close to the age of thirty-five. Yet he appeared maybe younger with short dark hair, intelligent onyx eyes, rugged face, and firm chin.

He was powerfully built. His chest and shoulders were broad and muscular, stretching the two-piece navy tunic he wore. Although he was born a prince, he was a trained athlete and excelled in rugby. His passion for sports had driven a national love for the game. So much so they'd fielded a team in the final stages of the recently concluded Rugby World Cup.

He was also an accomplished scholar and PhD holder, a patron dean of cultural studies at the University of Bagumi.

It was impossible not to be in awe of the man this close.

Unlike his sibling, who was constantly photographed with different women, Zawadi had rarely dated. In recent months he'd been pictured with a Nigerian princess. But there was no official announcement on his relationship status.

Whoever he married would be lucky to have a disciplined and fiercely driven man like Zawadi as a husband.

"I want to thank you for the work you did tonight and all the weeks leading up to it, Ms Ruga."

She blinked, realising the prince was addressing her directly while she'd been daydreaming about his relationship status. What was wrong with her?

"You're welcome, Your Highness," she managed to speak in a calm tone while her heart raced and her cheeks burned.

She met his gaze again and felt a sharp jolt to her heart, her chest squeezing tight in protest. It was like a thunderbolt of sensation—hot, electric. Her knees buckled, and her whole body felt weak. She was glad to be sitting.

For a moment, silence hung in the air, creating an intimate expectancy. She became warm and tingly as her gaze lowered to the sensuous curve of his mouth.

How would it feel to kiss those lips? Would they be firm, soft, or just right? What was he like as a lover? Would he carry the same dedication and passion he showed for other activities into the bedroom? What kind of sounds did he make while in the throes of pleasure?

The tingling spread from head to toes.

Goodness. What was wrong with her? She sat here, ogling the prince who was way out of her league. Despite how she was dressed tonight, she wasn't some delicate debutante or heiress who needed a charming prince to sweep her off her feet. She had nothing in common with the prince. Their worlds would never collide outside her official duty to the crown as a member of the Intelligence Service.

She was just feeling sex-starved and needed to get laid as soon as she returned to her everyday existence. Anyway, the prince was dating someone. So, she needed to quit gawking at him. Also, she'd been the one annoyed at the ostentatious luxury yacht earlier and thinking it was a waste of money. So, she shouldn't even like any person who showed off this kind of wealth.

With a rustle of fabric, Prince Zawadi rose from the sofa. "I know you must be tired. Stay the night and enjoy some rest and refreshments. You've all done a great job."

"Thank you, Your Highness." Razi stood as well, pulling Danai up with him.

The prince nodded, gave her that piercing stare again and strode out of the room.

Razi turned to her, a grin on his face. "You're drooling."

"Was not." Danai clamped her mouth shut, and her cheeks heated.

Razi just laughed at her and headed to the bar area as servants walked in with food trays.

There was no denying it. She had the hots for the crown prince.

# Chapter Four

Zawadi strode through the corridor towards the private cabin he needed.

This monstrosity of a luxury yacht was Zik's toy. To be more accurate, Zik shared ownership with two other friends.

Zawadi wasn't overly familiar with the yacht, although he had been aboard a few times previously. On this occasion, he'd needed a neutral location for the meeting with Kweku, and this was it.

Just like Zik had made the arrangements to capture Zawadi's former friend, he suggested using the yacht as the meeting point.

Zawadi had only flown out by helicopter to the yacht once Zik had received confirmation from the covert team about Kweku's capture. He couldn't delegate this part to his brother as well. This needed to be a face-to-face discussion. He would stare Kweku in the face as he got some answers.

Everything was going according to plan. So far. Zawadi wasn't foolish enough to ignore the potential for things to go wrong.

Mounting a covert mission in a friendly foreign country was a diplomatic nightmare. Capturing and taking a person across national borders without an appropriate warrant was another breach of international law.

Zawadi wouldn't sanction such activities under normal circumstances. He was about the rule of law and was a consummate diplomat.

Yet, here he was, doing the things he would have frowned upon. He was lucky to have the generosity and support of his siblings, especially Zik, who had taken the risk in setting up the mission in the first place.

Zik had volunteered to be here tonight. However, Zawadi had declined, needing to do this alone. Plus, he wanted to minimise the risk of things going wrong out here at sea.

Only a minimal number of people were aware of Zawadi's presence onboard this yacht. His siblings, Nathan, the yacht captain, and the helicopter pilot. They were all sworn to secrecy.

He'd arrived at the yacht not long before the captive had been brought onboard. The crew hadn't seen Zawadi disembark, only the captain. Therefore, the staff would assume Zik was here per usual, not Zawadi. Nathan ran interference, interacting with the others, so Zawadi didn't need to contact anyone else.

Also, to avoid an international incident, the yacht was cruising outside borders far away from land and territorial waters of the West African coastline. The nearest countries would be the Cape Verde Islands and Mauritania. In addition, there were fully equipped patrol boats to prevent pirates from gaining access to the vessel.

Now all Zawadi had to do was wait until the unconscious Kweku awakened. The man was currently secured in a cabin below deck where he would spend the night until the anaesthetic in his body wore off.

Zawadi glanced around the spacious cabin with furnishings, a vast bed and concealed cabinetry, finished in walnut-brown and leather and earthy tones. He supposed he could catch some sleep too. But his body and brain were too alert with excitement due to Kweku's capture.

His mind trailed to his meeting with the covert agents earlier.

He'd been informed when the boat showed up on the yacht's radar. Anticipation had flooded his system with adrenaline, and his heart had picked up speed. He'd already instructed Nathan to invite the agents onboard so he could meet them and thank them personally. The operatives had risked their jobs, lives, and freedoms to apprehend Kweku without official sanction from their bosses. If they'd been caught, they would have been disavowed and tagged as rogue agents.

It was only fair then for Zawadi to meet them personally, so they knew who'd sent them on such a risky mission. He was grateful for their brave actions.

However, he hadn't been prepared to see a woman in their midst.

It wasn't that he wasn't prepared to see a woman in their midst. He hadn't expected to see one looking as stunning as Ms Ruga in that dress.

Shaking his head, he removed the image of the beautiful female agent from his mind. He wouldn't entertain any distracting thoughts.

He should call Amara, his fiancée. But it was late, past midnight in Lagos, where she lived.

Amara's family, the Onohs, were close family friends and have been around through Zawadi's life. Her older brothers, Ejike, Ekene and Osita, were Zawadi's friends.

He hadn't interacted with Amara until she became Isha's best friend. Afterwards, she visited Darusa Palace frequently and came along to their family events.

Zawadi had always known his marriage would be arranged. Then when he was a young adult, his parents told him about the agreement between the Onohs and the Saenes for their children to wed to seal their continued friendship, which started many years ago in the 1960s.

Three months ago, Zawadi began courting Amara. For them, courtship wasn't a sexual dalliance. Instead, it was a process to build understanding and trust between them. The close ties between their royal houses meant they had shared values and a foundation for marital union. At the same time, their families would iron out the marriage contract.

Once the negotiations went past a certain point, their betrothal would be officially announced. His parents wanted the marriage contract completed within the year, if possible.

However, he wanted this Kweku issue out of the way first. Hence, the reason he was on this yacht tonight.

Sighing, Zawadi lowered his body into an armchair and tugged his shoes off. Then, he removed his clothes, walked into the adjoining bathroom for a shower before tugging on silk PJs.

Grabbing the case from the nightstand, he withdrew his reading glasses, picked his digital tablet from his overnight bag, and lowered his body into the armchair. Reading helped to calm his mind and aid his sleep.

He read a few chapters of a memoir, placed the device and spectacles on the bedside unit and climbed into the bed, tugging a sheet over his body. He flicked the light switch off, rolled to his side and was asleep minutes later.

The sound of the beeping phone alarm woke Zawadi.

Although this wasn't a typical working day, he rolled out of bed, padded to the bathroom for the ritual cleansing. Then he returned to the bedroom, found the prayer mat in a concealed cupboard. Using the compass on the bedside, he faced the correct direction and performed his dawn supplications. It didn't matter where he was. He always set his alarm to rise at the same time every day. Always followed the same routine.

Afterwards, he tugged on a pair of joggers, shoes and a t-shirt and took the short walk to the mini gymnasium. He walked through the opened door and stopped when he realised there was someone already using the room.

A woman was running on the machine, her trainers pounding on the treadmill.

It took him a few seconds to recognise her. Ms Ruga—one of the covert agents.

Her back was to him, and she wore headsets which meant she probably couldn't see or hear him. Her sweat-dampened grey t-shirt clung to her back, and the Lycra shorts showed off her round hips and curvy behind.

Desire punched him low in the gut, and heat skittered over his skin, catching him unawares.

Averting his gaze, he turned to retreat. He would have to find another way to exercise. Maybe a jog along the deck.

"Your Highness!"

Her exclamation made him glance back.

Looking surprised, she yanked her headphones down and decreased the running speed to a walking pace. "I'm sorry. I didn't realise you would be up this early. Did you need the machine? I'll get off."

There were other equipment he could use. For example, the cross-trainer, stepper, bike, or rower were great cardio options.

But the best way to resist temptation was to avoid it altogether. For all intents and purposes, he was betrothed to someone else. He didn't need trouble in the form of a near-naked female covert agent.

"No. Carry on, Ms Ruga. It's not a problem. You are free to use the facilities." He didn't wait for her response and walked away.

He returned to his cabin, deciding to abandon exercising altogether. Frustration made him kick his trainers off and stomp into the bathroom, turning the shower faucet to the cold setting.

His sudden spike in lust had to be because he'd been celibate since he started dating Amara. They had agreed to save sexual intercourse for their wedding bed.

Although his relationship with Amara wasn't about passion and sex, they were committed to each other. Their union would be an arrangement to seal a marriage contract between their families. Still, he'd promised to be faithful to her. To not look elsewhere for any kind of fulfilment.

He stepped into the glass enclosure, the cold-water pinpricks on his skin chasing away any remnant of his longing.

Ten minutes later, he was out, skin moisturised and tugging clothes on. The phone on the dresser buzzed, and he answered.

"Your Highness, the guest is awake," Nathan said.

"Good. Make him comfortable. I'll be there shortly," Zawadi replied before hanging up.

Excitement coursed through him as he finished dressing and headed out.

He strode into the reception lounge, where Kweku sat on a sofa.

"Good to see you awake," he said, standing by the entrance.

Kweku lifted his gaze. He appeared dishevelled, clothes askew. His eyes narrowed, and he pushed off the sofa. "Zawadi? Is that you?"

"The very same one," he said, walking into the room.

"Thank goodness." Kweku clutched his chest as a grin widened his face. He walked up to Zawadi and hugged him.

Zawadi didn't return the hug. Just patted the man on the back. In the corner of his eyes, he saw Nathan setting the table with the breakfast items and walking away.

Kweku stepped back, his grin widening. "Oh, you don't know how relieved I am. To wake up in a strange yacht with no memory of how I got here. For a moment, I imagined it was a Bahraini sheikh who owned it. I thought the man found out I fucked one of his wives and was going to cut my dick off or something. Rich enough to buy a country, but he is a sick bastard. Three wives, and he can't get it up to service any of them. Don't think any of the children are his too. The fucker."

Kweku laughed as he continued to ramble. "So, you bought a yacht. I always thought you were too much of a bloody scrooge but good on you for splurging out. When I get back to Wanai, it's one of the things I'm going to get myself. Buy a yacht the size of an island."

Zawadi flinched. Was Kweku serious? "You're going back to Wanai? Isn't there a warrant for your arrest?"

"That's nonsense. All hot air. There's nothing that I did that other governments around the world haven't done. So why am I being singled out?"

Zawadi walked over to the table where breakfast had been laid out. Was Kweku suffering from delusions? "You are accused of ethnic cleansing, which is a crime."

"False accusations because there was a coup. If I was in power, no one would accuse me of those things. They wouldn't dare." He sat on a chair and tucked into the plate of eggs benedict.

Zawadi sat opposite, lacking any appetite as he watched his former friend. "Are you saying you didn't order for the people of Ganuri to be massacred?"

Kweku lowered his cutlery and took a sip of the freshly squeezed grapefruit juice. "Look. I was dealing with terrorists. What was I supposed to do? Let them run the place? You know if it had been in Bagumi, you would have done the same thing?"

"No, I wouldn't. They were asking for a referendum and a chance to choose how they were governed. Instead, you used brutality, power blackouts, and internet shutdowns to hang on to power. You murdered peaceful civilians." Zawadi couldn't keep quiet. After what he had seen and heard, he never wanted to be compared to Kweku. He hoped he was a better, noble, and just leader.

Kweku's face clouded over. He chewed and swallowed, wiped his mouth, and flung the napkin on the table. "What the hell is this? Are you also accusing me?"

"I'm not. I just want to understand someone I regard as my friend." Zawadi placed his hands on the table. "You had a chance to be a better leader than your father. Yet you did worse things."

"Woah. Woah. Woah. Are you insulting my father now?" Kweku pushed his chair back, making it scrape against the hard flooring.

"I'm just stating the facts. Your father was voted into power over thirty years ago and has refused to let anyone else in, turning Wanai into his personal fiefdom, disregarding the people's right to choose."

Kweku's hard laughter filled the air. "That's rich coming from you. When was the last time the people of Bagumi got the right to choose their king?"

"You might not know this, but Bagumians get to choose their kings before the start of each reign. The king has to be given the consensus to rule."

"Yeah. Whatever." Kweku poured coffee into a porcelain cup, took it, and walked towards the glass window overlooking the rising golden sun and teal-blue ocean. "Where the hell are we, anyway?"

"In the middle of the Atlantic Ocean."

"Why?" He turned to face Zawadi.

"Because I needed to talk to you," Zawadi said. "I want to hear from you what happened between you and Isha ten years ago when she was a student in London."

"Why should I tell you? I'm sure she's already told you all kinds of stories."

"Tell me anyway. Because what you tell me will determine if I deliver you safely to Wanai or whether I call Sheikh Al-Farouk to pick you up." Although not a device he liked to use, Zawadi could be ruthless towards those who threatened the people he loved.

Kweku jolted, spilling hot black coffee on himself.

"Fuck," he cursed, reaching for a napkin to dab his shirt and trousers. He stared at Zawadi with wide, distressed eyes and swallowed. "You know Al-Farouk?"

It seemed Kweku was more scared of the sheikh than facing justice in his home country.

"Of course, I know Al-Farouk. We were all at Sandhurst together, remember?" Zawadi was disgusted that Kweku had stooped to having an affair with a married woman, the wife of their close friend. It went to show the man as dishonourable and untrustworthy. He was ashamed he had cared enough about Kweku to invite him to meet his family. He'd given consent for the man to date his sister, for goodness' sake.

Yet, the man had abused his trust and violated his sister.

Annoyance flared heat through his body, and he pulled the phone from his pocket as his patience ran out. "Get talking, Kweku or I'm calling Al-Farouk."

His old friend shifted uncomfortably. "You're really going to snitch on me? Zawadi, I'm your friend."

"And yet you did not respect our friendship. Tell me what you did to my sister. Now." He waved the phone.

"Fine," Kweku snarled. "Let me ask you a question. When you found out she was having an affair with her lecturer in London, how did you feel? Were you not angry?"

Zawadi crossed his arms over his chest. "Of course, I was. She was still so young. I felt the professor took advantage of her."

"Exactly. So, I did something about it. I broke them up. I threw his mother off a balcony, and she ended up in hospital." He tilted his head and gave a short laugh. "Of course, the professor had to return to Wanai. When he did, I detained him and tortured him until he promised never to see Isha again."

Zawadi narrowed his eyes. He needed to keep Kweku talking. He needed all the details. "You did?"

"Yes. It was so good inflicting pain on him and watching him suffer and break. He should never have touched Isha. He was beneath her." He paced up and down as he spoke. "Then I saw the email Isha sent to the professor, begging him to take her back. Telling him that she was pregnant. I was livid. How could she? How could she give her body to him? How could she carry his baby?"

Anger brewed inside Zawadi. He knew where this was going, but he fought to control his rage. He'd only found out about Isha's teenage pregnancy recently. She had kept it a secret from the family except for Zik and her mother, Queen Sapphire. Zawadi had only found out when they'd had a heart-to-heart conversation before she wedded the professor. She'd told him about the baby she'd lost many years ago.

Zawadi had been heartbroken for her for many reasons and mostly because she hadn't been able to confide in him back then. It had made him re-examine the way he related to his siblings and other people. He didn't want to be so far removed that they wouldn't trust him with their innermost troubles.

Which was why he needed to redeem himself by resolving this thing with Kweku.

"What did you do?" Zawadi asked in a cold voice.

"What else could I do? I couldn't let her have the bastard child. So, I had to get rid of it. You were visiting her in London at the time, and I tagged along because she never entertained me without you or Zik around. Anyway, I doctored her drink with a drug which would induce early labour—"

Zawadi grabbed a porcelain cup and smashed it against the hard floor, making Kweku jump. He was not usually prone to outbursts of violence. But he needed an outlet for the ball of rage in his gut. Otherwise, he might stoop to throwing the vile Kweku overboard. Then he would become no better than his former friend.

Instead, he clenched his fist around his phone as he dialled the number for his assistant. It was answered immediately.

"Tell the captain that we're headed to Boma," he said into the phone. "And instruct the men to secure Mr Doona in the hold until he is delivered to the Wanaian authorities."

"Yes, Your Highness," Nathan replied.

Zawadi ended the call and turned away.

"Don't do this. Come on. Just return me to Cape Verde. I'll grab my things and head off to a different country. You'll never see me or hear from me again. Please. You are my friend. The two of us are tight."

Zawadi met his gaze, his expression as cold and severe as he felt. "You are going back to Wanai to answer for your crimes. Be glad that I am nothing like you. Otherwise, I would have instructed the men to tie you to the anchor and throw you overboard so that your flesh will feed the fishes and your body never found. I am ashamed that I ever called you my friend."

Zawadi turned his back and walked away just as Nathan led armed men with cuffs and chains into the lounge from the second door.

# CHAPTER FIVE

*October 2019*

Zawadi sat in his office on the ground floor of the building that was the Offices of The Crown Prince of Bagumi. Directly outside the window was the circular courtyard with flowering shrubs. The sun was high in the sky, and the gardeners were busy trimming the hedges, the chopping of the clippers a gentle background sound.

Months ago, Kweku was handed over to the custody of the Wanaian authorities and the newly elected president, his brother-in-law, Professor Zain Bassong.

The day he'd spoken to Kweku, Zawadi called Isha and explained the package coming her way. Isha had been surprised because he hadn't mentioned his plan to locate Kweku to her. However, she'd been grateful and happy because having Kweku in secure custody meant the Wanaian people could finally get justice.

Kweku had since been arraigned, and a trial date had been set.

Zawadi was glad he didn't have Kweku's betrayal on his mind any longer. He'd made amends to Isha and the professor for his previous distrust and uncharitable actions.

Now he could focus on the future.

On a personal note, arrangements were ongoing for his traditional marriage to Amara in about nine months. They were officially engaged in modern terms. However, the Igbankwu ritual would entail his family travelling to Nigeria. To Amara's family home and formally asking for her hand in marriage. Since Amara's family were the host of the event, there was minimal involvement from Zawadi and his family at the preparatory stage.

Not such a tricky situation, compared to the current diplomatic issue giving him a headache. His brother, Zediah, had been betrothed to marry the daughter of the Barakat president, Bilkiss. Instead, Zed had married the love of his life, Riona, who'd already had a baby for him, Nour, that he hadn't known about until the child had been nine months old.

Unfortunately, this meant the Barakat government had ejected the Bagumi ambassador from Barakat, and tensions had risen between their anglers because of fishing rights and territorial waters.

Zawadi had a conference with said ambassador this morning about resolving the dispute. A marriage alliance between the two countries was now out of the question.

Suddenly a commotion broke out outside the window, and he heard Zareb shout, "Get down," before two blasts that sounded like gunshots.

Zawadi jerked upright as his door burst open, and his bodyguards ran in, immediately standing around him, shielding him.

"What's going on?" he asked, heart racing.

"There's an intruder. A shooter in the palace. Come with us."

As per the protocol during an emergency, Zawadi exited the office quickly, sandwiched between the guards and headed towards the safe room.

This was a fully equipped, bomb-proof, underground crisis bunker with no external windows. It had a backup power source, which kicked in case of an outage and a hidden door to a secret tunnel leading out of the palace.

On arrival, he unlocked the bunker door with his code and entered. There was almost the same floor space as the ground level of the building, with rooms for each royal family member and their staff.

However, Zawadi and his team were the only ones currently in here.

Luckily his parents were not in residence as they were at their Lake Miri home. Zed and his young family were on a visit to London. Zik was on a trip to Ethiopia and should be back tonight.

So, it was just him and Zareb, although Zareb didn't live at the palace.

"Where is Zareb?" he asked, reaching in his pocket for his phone.

One of the guards spoke into his earpiece before responding, "He is making the palace safe."

Zareb was the head of place security and was responsible for keeping the place and the people safe.

Zawadi nodded, pacing. He was unable to sit still while he didn't know what was going on. His heart was racing, adrenaline coursing through him. He hoped his brother was safe.

Thirty minutes later, the door popped open, and Zareb walked in.

Zawadi exhaled in relief as he hugged his brother. "What happened? Are you okay?"

"I'm fine," Zareb said. "An unknown assassin entered the palace grounds with a tourist group. He used a woman to create a diversion. He entered the private courtyard inside the office building disguised as a gardener. Unfortunately, his weapon was not detected by the scanner."

"What?" All his life, Zawadi had never encountered an assassin or ever heard of one breaching their defences. But to have one this close was chilling.

"It seems you were the target," Zareb's tone was sombre.

"Me?" Zawadi sat heavily into the chair.

"Yes. The gunman had secured a position directly opposite your office window with a clear view of you. He was taking aim when I shot him."

Zareb scrubbed a hand over his face. "He's dead. We're investigating to find out his accomplices. But, unfortunately, we don't know who else is involved in the conspiracy. So, we must be on the alert. For now, the palace is locked down."

Zawadi puffed out a breath. This was a shock. Someone had wanted him dead. Someone he didn't know. There could be others out there plotting his demise. For what reason?

The threat of assassination had always been something far removed. Some fantasy concept. A foreign idea. It had never affected him personally. He'd never thought it would be something he would worry about. He'd taken his security for granted if he was honest.

So, to be faced with this new reality that someone had planned a direct attack was a wake-up call and disheartening.

For the first time in his adult life, he felt … uncertain.

He had attended the Royal Military Academy in Sandhurst, had trained with some of the best in the world to become an army officer. Just like his father had done as a young man. He knew how to handle himself in a crisis and had served his country as part of the African peacekeeping troops in Darfur.

He had tackled drugs-stimulated militiamen who killed indiscriminately. Negotiated safe passage for the vulnerable old people, women, and children through war zones to protect innocent civilians. Come face to face with people pointing loaded weapons at him.

Yet, none of those situations had felt personal.

This one did. Someone wanted Zawadi, specifically, to die.

"What now?" he asked the question in his mind. He had never been in this situation before, and nothing had prepared him for it.

"I need to get back to the security offices and go through the CCTV images to find out if there are any accomplices. Can you call Papa and let him know the situation? You're better at conveying this kind of news to him. Also, if you could speak to Zik."

"Sure. I'll get to that. Do you want me to speak to Zed too?"

"No. I'll speak to him."

After Zareb left, Zawadi got on his phone and made the necessary phone calls. Keeping busy took his mind off the shocking implications of the attack.

Afterwards, he got a briefing from Zareb. The woman who had caused the distraction during the tourists' visit had been apprehended. Apparently, she had been recruited by the attacker that morning and paid money to generate the distraction. There was nothing in her history linking her to a terrorist group. However, she had been released. Her movements would be monitored in the next few days until they could clear her from the investigations.

The palace press coordinator worked on the media statement, which read:

There had been an incident at Darusa Palace. Investigations were ongoing.

After that, Zawadi gave a press briefing to confirm that members of the royal family were doing well.

By the time the day was gone, he was mentally exhausted.

Yet when he went to bed, he couldn't sleep.

# CHAPTER SIX

*December 2019*

Danai rolled the motorbike down the narrow gap between the buildings and parked it in the shed she used as a lockup. Then she unstrapped her overnight bag, hauled it over her shoulder, and walked out to the high street pavement.

The sky was overcast, the afternoon sun breaking through grey clouds in patches. Across the busy, tarred bi-directional road stood a double-fronted shop with bright yellow board and bold black lettering proclaiming 'Mou Supermart'.

A full-figured woman in a maxi black and orange print dress stepped out of the shop, saw Danai and waved enthusiastically. She looked left and right, checking for oncoming vehicles. When it was clear, she jogged across the street.

"Danai, good to see you." They embraced, and Danai was cocooned in soft curves and jasmine fragrance.

"Same here. How are you?" She leaned back, smiling and checking the woman out. "You look fab as usual, by the way."

"Me well, *mèsi.*" A beautiful smile curled Oumou's lips. "How about you? How long are you visiting?"

"For the weekend."

"Oh, good, because I have to rush somewhere. But I'll see you later."

"Of course. See you later."

They embraced briefly, and Oumou hurried back across the street. Her friend spoke to a teen girl in a mauve and white school uniform before getting into the yellow pickup van with the shop logo emblazoned on the sides.

Oumou started the car engine and waved as she drove past. "*Akeyi lakay ou*, Danai."

"*Mèsi*," Danai thanked her, waving back.

She'd known Oumou since they were children when they hung around their parents' businesses after school. Danai at her dad's mechanic garage and Oumou across the street in her mother's convenience shop. They'd attended the same high school. But when Danai had applied to university afterwards, her friend had chosen to stay at the local college instead.

Oumou hadn't been academically inclined. But she had a great business brain and had since expanded her mother's store from a simple provisions' shop to a medium-sized self-service grocery and household retail outlet. The main one in their small town.

Danai loved seeing her friend be a boss lady. But she was also her stepsister because Danai's father had married Oumou's mother a few years ago.

Now, Danai swivelled in the opposite direction. An assortment of damaged cars stood on the unpaved forecourt in various stages of repair. The sound of an electric drill clashed with music blasting from a radio and a running car engine.

She avoided the puddles of rainwater as she walked towards the bays where men in oil-stained overalls worked on vehicles on ramps and lifts. The smell of grease, petrol and metal floated in the air.

The scents and sounds filled her with nostalgia, and a smile broke on her face. It didn't matter where else in the world she'd visited or the calibre of people she'd met. This was home. Where she truly belonged.

One of the men swivelled, probably expecting to see a customer.

"Danai!" he cheered, and the rest of the men turned in her direction, calling out greetings.

"Hello, guys," she replied, smiling.

"Hey, ti sè," the first guy, her cousin, wrapped her in a familial hug. "We weren't expecting you today."

"Hey, Yahya. I thought I'd make it a surprise." She untangled from him and patted his stubbled chin. "You know you're only a few months older than me, right?"

At thirty years old, Yahya was her oldest cousin, the son of her father's brother, Uncle Hissene. He had a sister, Aminata, who would turn twenty-five this year.

"I'm still older, coz." Yahya took her travel bag and carried it towards the cabin, which served as the office. "How's work?"

"Work's good." She walked past the small wooden reception counter to the chair in front of a dark-wood table and settled into it. "I have a few days between assignments, so I decided to visit you guys."

"You missed us." Her cousin grinned and leaned against the desk. The top half of his blue overall was wrapped around his hips, revealing a white cotton vest clinging to and contrasting against bulging ebony muscular chest, shoulders, and arms.

Danai chuckled. "I did. Where is dad?"

"My dad picked yours up earlier. They had a meeting in the city."

"Oh. I guess I'll see him later. How are Uncle and Auntie and Aminata."

Her dad, Ngarta, and Yahya's father, Hissene, were brothers. The two of them had started the mechanic shop when they'd been young men. But Hissene decided to go into local politics years ago and was now a regional council member.

"Everyone is fine. Pops is still giving me a hard time about working here. Thinks I should come work with him."

"Doing what? You love dismantling cars and putting them back together."

Uncle Hissene had been trying to convince her dad to leave the auto shop and join him in politics. But her father was a simple man who loved the simple life. So, imagine Hissene's dismay when his son decided he wanted to work as a mechanic.

"I don't even know for Pops. I have no interest in sitting in an office and getting fat."

He chuckled as she shook her head in amusement.

"There are things I would compromise but not that." Yahya's eyes glazed in a faraway expression.

Danai could imagine what her cousin was thinking. "I was saying hello to Oumou just now."

He flinched but quickly tried to cover his response by turning away.

"Okay. How is she?" he asked in a nonchalant voice as he walked to the small fridge in the corner.

She wasn't fooled. The mention of Oumou's name always got a reaction from him. There was something between Yahya and Oumou, but her cousin would not admit it.

"She is fine. But you should know that already. She's just across the road. All you have to do is stroll over to check on her."

He grabbed a re-used plastic water bottle, poured water into two glasses, and handed one to her.

"I don't see much of her. It's been busy over here." He pointed at the lot filled with cars in various stages of repair.

"Well, hopefully, you can take a break this weekend, and we can all hang out and catch up," she said before taking a sip of the refreshing liquid.

The three of them had been thick as thieves. Because Yahya, Oumou and Danai were close in age, they'd attended school, done chores, and played together.

Until hormones, growing up, and life had gotten in the way.

Danai, more than Oumou, had been rambunctious and had played sports with the boys, whether soccer or rugby. She'd done whatever her cousin had done, climbed rocks, raced on bicycles, swam in the lake.

Oumou had stopped doing those things when they became teenagers, suddenly not wanting to get dirty and behaving strangely around Yahya. It was years later before Danai realised Oumou was attracted to Yahya. She could swear her cousin felt the same thing towards their childhood friend, but neither person had done anything about it, as far as she knew.

"Yes, of course, we'll do something. The lads and I are going to a new bar in Wandjoun tomorrow night. You're welcome to join us."

They were in Bali, a small town in the north-eastern region of Bagumi with a population of less than three thousand. The people spoke a mix of Creole and French, although many also spoke English, which was the official language.

About thirty minutes' drive to the west was the regional capital Wandjoun, where Uncle Hissene lived with Yahya's mother and sister. Yahya stayed in Danai's family home during the week to be closer to the mechanic shop.

Another sore point between Yahya and his father because her cousin was living away from home. Although Danai knew her aunt was pleased Yahya wasn't bringing home car grease and petrol stench every night. She was intent on climbing the social ladder. So, whenever Yahya went home, he was scrubbed clean and looking presentable, just in case his parents had guests.

"Sure. I'd love to join you." She was pleased he still saw her as one of the lads, which was how his friends had always treated her. "Can I invite Oumou too?"

"If you want to." He shrugged.

"Great. I'll message her. Woohoo! The Beautiful, The Bold and The Brave will ride again." She raised her glass, grinning.

Yahya chuckled, shaking his head. "You still remember that."

"Of course, I remember," she replied.

A horrible teacher had once called them The Good, The Bad and The Ugly in front of the class, implying that Yahya was The Bad because he struggled with academics and Oumou was The Ugly because she was chubby.

Furious, Danai had stood and defended her cousin and her friend, retorting, "Sir, you're wrong. We are The Beautiful—" she'd pointed at Oumou because her friend was the most gorgeous soul inside and out "—The Brave—" she'd indicated Yahya. Although he struggled, he never gave up and still turned up to school every day working as hard as anyone else to learn "—and The Bold—" she'd dropped her hand. Well, she had been courageous for challenging the teacher when she knew he would penalise her.

The punishment had been swift. Detention and cutting a patch of grass on the school field. Yahya had later told Danai while helping her cut the grass that she was The Brave in their outfit because of how she'd stood up to the bully teacher.

She'd ended up with blistered palms, but she had no regrets and hadn't been deterred. She would always stand up for the victim against bullies in whatever form they came in later life.

This had been part of her motivation to join the Bagumi Intelligence Service when she'd attended their careers event at university—protecting the vulnerable from those who would exploit them. Of course, it helped that she was naturally friendly and seemed to engender trust in others. She had empathy and could entertain and understand complex and contradicting concepts of rectitude.

Just then, voices drew her attention to the main floor, and she swivelled.

She recognised the tall, lean, handsome man in his mid-fifties wearing grey linen tunic and trouser suit, black shoes and walking towards the office.

"Dad." She stood, hurrying to the door.

"Danai?" Her father paused mid-stride before a grin broke on his sepia-hued clean-shaven face. He opened his arms wide, and she stepped into his tight hug.

She leaned back. He stared at her with dark amber eyes and a genial smile. Low silver-brown tightly curled hair covered his head.

"This is a wonderful surprise. When did you arrive?" He glanced past her towards where Yahya stood. "Did you know she was coming?"

"I was surprised too when she showed up about forty minutes ago," her cousin replied.

Her father's forehead wrinkled. "Is everything okay?"

"Everything is okay. Can't I just come home whenever I want? This is still my home, isn't it?" she teased, giving her dad a side hug.

"Of course, it's your home. You can come home whenever you want. It's just that you always call before you return."

He had a point. She'd booked the trip back after she'd been given the file for her new assignment. She'd been unnerved, conflicted, not because of the job itself but the person involved.

She'd come home because when she needed solace, this was where she got it. Her father was her hero, her champion, her most significant cheerleader.

He'd always told her to be herself and speak her mind even when other people wanted to suppress her. She'd been tagged as 'too boisterous' or 'she wasn't behaving like a girl.'

For example, after the teacher had punished her for correcting him in class, she'd come home, her father had applied ointment to her blisters and spoken to her.

"Were you rude to the teacher?" he'd asked. When she'd said "no", he told her that the world was full of people like the teacher. So, she should be prepared to fight and go through inconveniences in the pursuit of justice and fairness.

"Nothing comes easy in life, Danai. There will always be a sacrifice. Be prepared to make them."

She'd kept his words to heart all these years. But she didn't want to discuss the matter that had brought her home yet. So, she changed the subject. "This semi-retirement is good for you. You seem to be getting younger."

He'd handed over most of the managerial responsibilities to Yahya, who was now in charge of the mechanic shop.

Her father's laughter boomed. "Nothing beats a simple, stress-free life."

"And the love of a good woman," Yahya chimed in with a grin.

"That too." Dad chuckled. "Let's go home. Mama Oumou would be happy to see you."

Danai had to agree.

Danai's parents had divorced when she was little. Her mother remarried and moved to another country. For many years, her father had focused on his business and his daughter. He hadn't dated or remarried, although his brother had practically nagged him to do so, saying there needed to be a woman in his life to raise Danai and bear him sons.

"Danai is both my son and my daughter," he would say. And she had loved him more for sticking up for her and not caving to her uncle's misogyny. She had sworn to always make her father proud of her and her life choices.

Now, her father seemed so much happier since he married Oumou's mother's whose husband died when Oumou was a young girl. He wasn't working so hard anymore and was enjoying life with his new spouse.

***

Rolling, sedate, green plantation fields gave way to the energetic city as pavements, buildings, and traffic jams took over on the drive from the airport to Darusa Palace.

Danai watched the rapidly moving scenery without retaining much.

Last week, she'd been called into a meeting by her superiors and told that she had been assigned a new case.

Three weeks ago, an armed man had entered a private courtyard in the palace and had attempted to kill Crown Prince Zawadi.

When Danai had heard the news, her blood had run cold.

Sure, she didn't know the crown prince personally, but he was still a much-loved member of the Bagumi royal family.

Aside from the encounter on the yacht months ago, after they apprehended Kweku Doona, she hadn't seen him again. There'd been a brief conversation in the gymnasium. Then, the yacht had docked briefly while she and Razi had been dropped off that same morning.

Then one evening, she heard the news about the failed assassination in a TV broadcast.

Thankfully, Prince Zareb had shot and killed the attacker. Further investigations showed the man may have had accomplices, but none had been apprehended so far.

Most critical was the idea that one of the accomplices was either a palace employee or a royal family member involved in the conspiracy to murder Prince Zawadi. Therefore, an insider passed on vital information detailing the exact location of the crown prince's office and his whereabouts at the time. Even the idea that the security scanners missed the man's loaded weapon indicated that someone turned a blind eye at the right moment.

Somebody close to the prince wanted him dead.

That concept filled Danai with as much horror as rage.

Now Danai had been tasked with finding out who in the palace was involved.

Her hand clenched on her lap. First, she would find the person who was betraying Prince Zawadi's trust and committing treason. Then, they would pay for their crimes.

She sat in the car on the way to the palace to start her new assignment.

The Bagumi Intelligence Service had been tasked by parliament to head the investigations since this was a national security problem.

She was under no illusion that this would be an easy investigation. The conspirators had gone to great lengths to hide their actions. Hence, she had to go undercover as Prince Zawadi's personal guard.

This was the only way to stay close to him and have free access to the palace, employees, visitors, and residents.

She flexed her fingers as nervous energy roiled through her. She couldn't wait to get started.

"Are you excited about starting a new job?" the man beside her in the driver's seat asked.

A slight annoyance at the distraction from her thoughts, she glanced at the man who had introduced himself as Yusuf. He hadn't said much since he picked her from the house in Bali this morning.

She'd enjoyed the weekend spent with her people, a night out with Yahya and Oumou on Saturday and a countryside ride on her beloved motorbike on Sunday.

*"I'm proud of you,"* her father had spoken those words, beaming with a smile before she dragged her bag to the waiting dark SUV outside. He thought being assigned to the palace was prestigious for her and the family.

Although Uncle Hissene was a member of the regional council, he'd never met any members of the royal house, to her knowledge. Danai would be the first person in her family to meet and work directly for the RF.

"Danai?" Yusuf's voice jerked her to the present.

It took a second to remember his question. "Yes, I'm looking forward to the new job."

"Good. It is a thing of prestige to serve our great country's royal family."

"It is. So how long have you worked at the palace?" she asked. She'd read files about the palace security team. She knew Yusuf's history at the palace but wanted to gauge his personality.

"Five years," he said, weaving in and out of the terrible traffic. "Have you met the royal family before?"

The mention of the royal family made her stomach clench. She'd met famous celebrities while undercover. Yet, there was something different about meeting the royal family. They were in a different league. As demonstrated by the prince when she'd met him months ago.

"Not all of them. I met Prince Zawadi briefly once." She kept to the truth. Even when undercover, it was best to stick to the fact wherever possible.

Prince Zawadi sitting on the sofa like a king on the night they met, played in her mind. She didn't know a lot about the prince other than what she'd read about him. But one thing was sure, even the thought of him made her core clench and her pulse rate increase. The strength of the attraction to him still shocked her.

The car circled the roundabout with the statue of the first king of modern Bagumi and onto the four-lane Regents Avenue leading to Darusa Palace, which loomed large in the distance.

Yusuf slowed the car as they approached the checkpoint. He lowered the window and greeted the guards. They nodded at Danai, went around the vehicle with the scanners, checking the boot and underneath before clearing them to drive in.

At the top of the palace, the flags flew high, indicating that the royal family were in residence. Knots constricted her throat. She would be seeing Prince Zawadi again soon.

Yusuf drove down a private lane away from the public area. He pulled into the car park marked 'staff only'.

"Welcome to Darusa Palace," Yusuf said, unclipping his seatbelt and reaching for the door.

"Thank you." She did the same and stepped out of the car into bright sunshine. "Can I leave my bag in the car and pick it up later."

She was supposed to meet the prince straight away and didn't want to drag her luggage around.

He opened the boot and took the small suitcase out. "I'll put the bag in the staff storeroom, and you can pick it later."

"Okay. That's great. Thank you." She took the handle and followed him up a ramp and through double doors that led into a corridor.

He opened another door. "You can put it in here."

It was a storeroom with shelving, mostly empty. Danai stowed the bag in a corner. "Thanks again."

"No problem. This way." He moved along the winding vaulted corridors, her shoes clicking on the polished marble floor. Then across a courtyard with beautiful colourful flowers into another hallway with ornate ceilings reached two stories high with large crystal chandeliers dotting every twelve feet. Fifteen-foot gold-trimmed mirrors lined the wall reflecting marble statues, rococo-style chairs, and benches upholstered in deep purple silk.

Matching drapes accented the massive windows, and fresh flowers sat in ornament vases on several tables. Everything was exquisite, refined, and stunning, a mix of elegance and luxury. But, of course, it was a palace.

Up a grand staircase, through another set of double doors and past more stationary guards, Yusuf pointed at a room. "You should wait in here. The prince will be with you shortly."

"Thanks again for coming to pick me up, Yusuf," she said. The palace had sent a car to pick her because unauthorised vehicles were not allowed at the premises since the assassination attempt. However, since she didn't own a car, she couldn't have taken a taxi.

Her job meant she was rarely home and didn't need a car. Even when she was at head office, she used official vehicles. However, she couldn't use BIS pool cars for the job at the palace.

"Sure. You're welcome. I'll see you later." He turned and walked away.

She stepped inside. This was a reception room with velvet sofas, soft carpets, and sheer drapes. More flowers stood in a vase on a table by the window.

Choosing not to sit, she examined the paintings and sculptures. Then she walked up to the window and gasped.

The view was amazing. The morning sunshine lit the palace gardens and the cityscape. New skyscrapers stood alongside old landmarks. Towers stood against rolling hills. Directly ahead was the magnificent view of Regents Avenue with the cars and pedestrians going about their lives.

"And you are?"

The eloquent female voice had Danai swivelling swiftly.

"Your Majesty," she curtsied when she recognised Queen Zulekha in all her gorgeous and flawless splendour.

This was Zawadi's mother.

Dressed in a deep blue ankle-length silk dress and silver heels, the queen was tall and lean, with the most delicate swan neck and dainty wrists. Her hair was wrapped in an embroidered turban. She had a wide mouth, hazel eyes, and high cheekbones, and she oozed elegance like it was a perfume she put on.

The daughter of a nobleman, she'd been raised to be a queen. And as the first wife of King Ibrahim, she was the formal consort. Rumour had it that although the king wanted to marry someone else, her family had blackmailed the king into marrying her.

Danai didn't know how accurate those rumours were by staring at the queen's calculating eyes. She remembered the question.

"I'm Danai Ruga, Your Grace."

"You're my son's new bodyguard?" Queen Zulekha raised her eyebrow.

How did the woman know?

"Yes, Your Grace."

"Hmmm." The royal said, her forehead wrinkled in a frown. "Carry on."

The queen walked off in a flurry of fabric.

Danai got the distinct feeling the woman hadn't been impressed by her.

She sighed, shaking off the disappointment. She wasn't here to impress the royal family.

She was here to catch a traitor.

# CHAPTER SEVEN

Zawadi caught himself glancing at his gold watch for what seemed like the hundredth time today and grimaced. He'd been doing that a lot in the past month, since the assassination attempt on his life.

He found himself getting distracted and not concentrating, especially in meetings.

He hadn't been himself.

This meeting was about recent skirmishes between Bagumi and Barakat fisher people.

Ever since his brother Zediah reneged on his betrothal to the daughter of the Republic of Barakat's president, tensions had risen again. The same conflicts had been brewing for years between the neighbouring countries.

Over a year ago, a deal was brokered between the two. It was agreed that King Ibrahim's son would marry the president's daughter to foster a closer relationship between the two countries.

Unfortunately, Zediah fell in love with another woman he'd met in London and married her. However, Zed wouldn't see it as unfortunate because he was happily married.

Meanwhile, the happy union of the two countries had descended into squabbles by anglers.

First, Barakat had ejected the Bagumian ambassador in protest of Bagumi pulling out of the deal. Now, their citizens were almost coming to blows out in the territorial waters.

Zawadi had been in a conference about this issue for the past hour with the Permanent Secretary to the Forestry and Fisheries Commission.

He would rather be discussing a cultural or educational issue which was his forte. However, because this had descended into a diplomatic matter, the problem was squarely at his door.

"So let me get this right. Bagumian fishers accuse their Barakat counterparts of using aggressive trawlers for fishing in the territorial water. And Barakat anglers say they are not responsible because the trawlers belong to the Chinese?"

"Yes, that sums it up." Mr Naako replied.

"Do we have proof that Chinese trawlers are fishing our waters?" he asked.

"No. Just anecdotes."

"Okay. Nathan—" he turned to his assistant who was taking notes "—please arrange a call with the head of Naval Border Patrol, so we can investigate this further. Also, arrange a cabinet meeting and include Mr Sembene to discuss the diplomatic problems with Barakat at the earliest opportunity."

Mr Sembene was the recalled Bagumian ambassador for Barakat.

"Yes, Your Highness," Nathan replied, tapping on the tablet device on the table.

"Mr Naako, thank you for bringing this to my attention." Zawadi stood, making the other man stand too. "Reassure our fishermen that we're working to resolve this issue."

"Of course, Your Highness. Thank you for your time." The man bowed.

"You're welcome. I'll be in touch soon." Zawadi nodded.

Nathan held the door to the conference room. Zawadi walked out first, followed by the commissioner. The man headed down the stairs with Nathan. Zawadi strode towards his office across the foyer on the same floor. He pulled his phone out of his pocket to check his messages.

To the left was the see-through glass wall separating the gallery-style offices from the foyer. On the right was the elevator for those who didn't want to use the stairs.

Just ahead was his office suite.

A protection officer in a grey trouser suit stood in an alert stance by the wall, feet wide apart, hands clutched at the back, head still, eyes scanning the space.

Goosebumps skittered over Zawadi's skin, and he halted, momentarily stunned.

It was *her*. The covert agent. She was here, in the palace, staring at him with bright, brilliant eyes that seemed to see everything.

Their gazes locked, and he forgot everything else for a few seconds.

Adrenaline flushed through his body, and his heart raced.

The sound of an opening door brought him to his senses.

What was she doing here?

Ignoring her, Zawadi walked towards his office. He didn't care why she was here.

"Your Highness." Ms Ruga curtsied as he went past.

"Ms Ruga." He nodded but didn't look at her.

"Hold up," Zareb stepped out of one of the offices, striding towards him.

"What's going on?" Zawadi asked, chin tilted to the woman who hadn't moved from the spot behind his brother.

"In your office," Zareb said, indicating for Zawadi to go first. "Ms Ruga, you can come in too."

Zawadi entered, stopped in the middle of the spacious room, and swivelled towards the entrance. The prickling on his spine forewarned he wouldn't like the conversation with his brother. So, he stiffened, steeling his mind.

His brother entered, followed by the woman, who stopped beside Zareb after closing the door.

Expression blank, Zareb stepped into the middle of the group like a mediator. "This is Ms Ruga from the BIS. She has been assigned as your new principal protection officer."

PPO? She was his new head bodyguard. No.

"Why?" he asked, unable to stop himself.

"You're aware that BIS are investigating the assassination plot," Zareb said.

"Yes?"

"They believe there is a co-conspirator in the palace."

"There is?"

"Your Highness," Ms Ruga spoke before his brother could reply. "There is evidence to suggest someone in the palace passed on information about the layout and the location of your office."

"Or it could be someone who has visited the offices and met with the crown prince," his brother said in a stern voice.

Zawadi could imagine that Zareb would not be pleased that his operations as head of palace security were under scrutiny by an external body.

"An investigation will eliminate the innocent suspects. That's why I'm here," Ms Ruga said.

"Are you suggesting that my team are not investigating?" Zareb narrowed his eyes, his anger barely concealed by his tight jaw.

"No. That's not what I meant. I'm just here to do a job," Ms Ruga said, softly although her demeanour said she would not back down.

"Yes, remember that you're an employee," Zareb snapped.

It wasn't like his brother to lose his temper. But the assassination attempt had frayed everyone's nerves, it seemed.

"Reb, it's okay," Zawadi used his brother's nickname, stepping up to calm the situation. He waved at the sofas. "Ms Ruga, please take a seat."

The agent walked around and settled on the sofa, her back to them. She looked composed despite his brother's words.

Zareb's chest rose and fell as he took a deep breath. "It seems you know Ms Ruga."

Zawadi's skin prickled as he sighed. He should know he couldn't hide anything from the ever-observant Zareb.

"Yes, Ms Ruga was part of the team that apprehended Kweku when he was a fugitive. I met her on the yacht."

His brother's eyes narrowed, and he tilted his head to the side and moved away from the sofa section towards the windows. Zareb leaned his head towards his brother's and lowered his voice. "I thought we agreed very few people should know you were on that yacht."

"I know. But I wanted to thank the team who put their careers in jeopardy to bring Kweku to justice."

"Hmmm. You should've told me this when you got back. Who else was there?"

"Just Mr Hamadou, Zik's friend."

"I don't like it. But let's hope they don't try to cash in on that bit of news."

They both glanced in Ms Ruga's direction. She hadn't moved from the spot.

His brother implied the covert agent would sell the news to the media about Zawadi's involvement in Kweku's capture. Or use it for social media clout and clicks.

Somehow, Zawadi didn't believe she would do such a thing. For one, she hadn't revealed to Zareb, who was his brother, that she had met Zawadi already. Second, she'd risked a lot for the mission, her career and possible imprisonment for abducting Kweku without a warrant. Also, it had been a few months. If she'd wanted to sell the story, she would have done so already.

Despite not wanting Ms Ruga here or as his new PPO, Zawadi couldn't help coming to her defence. "I think we can trust her."

Zareb jerked. "Why do you think so?"

"Instinct. She comes across as competent and smart. Also, I think she will find the mole if there is one in the palace. We all want that, so go easy on her."

Zareb sighed. "Fine. I'll give her space to do her job. Mind you, you're the one she'll be shadowing, so—" he raised both palms facing forwards, implying that Ms Ruga was Zawadi's headache "—anyway, must go. Taking our number one queen to her six-monthly women's initiative meeting."

"Sure. Later," Zawadi said.

Zareb walked towards the door. "See you later, Ms Ruga."

"Bye, Your Highness," she replied.

Zawadi strode to the sofas and lowered his body onto the one opposite Ms Ruga as Zareb shut the door behind him.

She stiffened, sitting upright, and meeting his gaze.

One thing he'd give the BIS agent, she didn't cower easily, and her gaze didn't flick away coyly like other women did in his presence.

He'd seen her in three different outfits, a ballgown, a sports kit and this formal suit and tie. Each time she looked different. And yet familiar.

There was something about her...

*What are you doing?* The voice in his head pulled him from his wandering thoughts. Kept him grounded in the now.

"How long?" he asked, keeping his voice and expression devoid of emotion.

"Your Highness, I don't understand the question," she said, forehead furrowing in a frown.

"I mean, how long are you going to be—" he hesitated for a beat as he chose the right words "—working at the palace."

He avoided asking how long she was going to be his bodyguard. That would have made it seem personal when this was a professional situation, and she was on a mole-hunt. The PPO bit was just her cover.

"As long as it takes to find the palace spy. Then I'll be out of your hair," she said in a weighted tone as if she appreciated he didn't want her here.

"Good. Well, thank you, Ms Ruga. You can return to your duties." He stood, dismissing her, and strode towards his desk.

"Your Highness, one more thing," her smooth voice held authority. Like she was commanding him to stop.

Hmm? Didn't she understand that he had dismissed her already? That she couldn't reverse it.

No one commanded him except for his father, the king.

Around here, in the palace especially, he gave orders, and everyone else obeyed.

Yet, he halted and swivelled. Body stiffened, one brow raised, he hardened his tone. "Ms Ruga?"

She stood and met his gaze without flinching, hands clasped in front. "The positioning of your desk is too close to the window and gives a sniper direct access to you. I'd like to request moving your desk over to this side of the room and moving the sofas over there."

For some reason, her request irritated him.

Maybe because it was another thing linked to the assassination attempt, which had become the bane of his life in the past few weeks. It was bad enough he'd had to change so much about his life since the event.

As it was, he couldn't shake the sense of impending doom, as if his life was disintegrating and he couldn't pull it together.

He'd already relocated his office from the ground floor space he used previously to this one after the incident. He didn't need any more rearrangements. The window was bulletproof anyway. Zareb had them all changed recently.

"No, Ms Ruga," he said in a cold voice. "Your request is denied. You're dismissed."

He turned his back to her, strode to his desk and sat in the brown leather armchair. Not looking at the woman, he opened his laptop and logged into the network.

His heart thumped against his ribs as the seconds ticked by before he heard the door shut with a click, announcing Ms Ruga's departure.

He tipped his head back, blew out air. This was turning into one of those days, those weeks, those months.

He was a prince, the crown prince of the Kingdom of Bagumi. His responsibilities were immense, and he couldn't allow himself to be distracted by an assassination attempt or the woman sent to investigate it.

He counted to five, cleared his mind and focused on the next item on his seemingly never-ending to-do list.

# CHAPTER EIGHT

Danai was quickly learning that life as a PPO was about routine.

On Monday, after her brief encounter with Queen Zulekha in the Safari reception room, Yusuf returned and escorted her to Zareb's office in the security suite.

During the meeting, Prince Zareb's animosity had been blatant. He didn't like having his authority overruled by the Bagumi Intelligence Service, who had sent her as a semi-permanent feature at the palace until the assassination conspirators were found.

As if it was Danai's fault. She was an employee of His Majesty's Secret Service, sent by her superiors to investigate a matter of national security.

Damn, if she wasn't going to do her job and do it as best as she could, come Hell or high water.

Still, she'd been glad when the meeting with Prince Zareb had ended. Yusuf had shown her around the control room with all the CCTV monitors and the computers tracking palace activities and assets. She'd viewed the layout of the critical areas of the palace. Then he'd taken her to her studio residence in the staff quarters.

Finally, he'd brought her to the Crown Prince's office suites. He informed her to wait because Prince Zawadi was in a meeting. She'd stood there waiting. Until she'd heard the door to the conference room open and Prince Zawadi exited first followed by a man she didn't recognise, then Nathan.

The crown prince looked magnificent as always. His broad shoulders stretched the navy vest over the white long-sleeved shirt and silver tie, his long legs in navy trousers and brown brogues. The platinum cufflinks on his wrists caught the light and glittered. He had a gadget in his hand and was flicking his long fingers across the screen.

Adrenaline had rushed through her. She'd become breathless, and her senses heightened.

He walked towards her, and her pulse raced. He would be close to her any minute.

Then he looked in her direction, and her heart thumped so hard she feared he would hear its drum-like beats.

He seemed confused, at first, eyebrows squished together. Yet, he didn't break the gaze or ask any questions.

His eyes searched her face. It was as if they were interlocked, bound together, everything else frozen out.

She'd never experienced anything like it—how the intensity of his gaze robbed her of breath.

A sound broke the spell. He continued walking, going past her towards his office.

Was he going to ignore her?

She greeted him, and he curtly acknowledged her.

Seemed he wasn't altogether pleased about her presence either. And he hadn't known she would be there.

Okay. Danai could understand his aloof demeanour.

His brother turned up then, and they all went into Prince Zawadi's office.

Zareb had explained the situation, and Crown Prince Zawadi had shown his irritation.

Still, when his brother had gotten annoyed and pulled rank, reminding her that she was just an employee, the crown prince had defended her.

Which had warmed her heart. Zawadi was a kind and fair man. It seemed he didn't like anyone being maltreated.

The brothers stepped away to chat in low voices. She didn't quite hear, although she could guess at what they discussed. Her.

Then Prince Zareb had left the office, and it had been just her and Prince Zawadi.

She'd remained calm while he sat on the sofa, although her heart had been racing.

Even while sitting, he still looked regal.

During their brief conversation, she'd deduced that he'd accepted her presence, although he wasn't altogether happy about it.

Relieved that she could get on with doing her job, she'd asked to have his office rearranged to minimise the risk of another attack on the crown prince.

And he'd shut her down without an explanation.

That had pissed her off.

Her primary assignment was to keep Prince Zawadi safe. It meant being a protective barrier between him and anyone intending to harm him. Her job involved doing risk assessments about every location the prince would visit, including his workplace and residences.

She'd assessed his office while the brothers had been chatting and had found it hadn't been arranged in the safest way. It wasn't the worst. Neither was it the best.

Still, there was nothing she could do but leave the prince's presence after he'd dismissed her. She would have to work out another way of rearranging the office.

So, she'd stood outside his office for the rest of the day. The earpiece in her left ear helped her communicate with the other guards in her team. Someone took her place when she needed to use the ladies or stop for a quick snack.

Luckily, the prince had no outside engagements on the first day, so they hadn't left the palace. However, the evening, she had walked alongside him as he returned to his residence, an apartment on the other side of the sprawling palace.

She had opened the door with her keyset while the prince waited. Then she walked inside and checked all the rooms to make sure there wasn't an intruder. Then, satisfied the place was clear, she bid him goodnight.

She left the night guards outside his door while she did the long walk to her one-bed studio in the staff quarters. Dinner was in the staff canteen, although she could have gone into town if she'd been inclined.

Instead, she'd sat in bed, typing her report on the laptop while the TV was on in the background. There hadn't been much to report. She'd just made observations about the people she'd interacted with, omitting the supercilious Queen Zulekha, the indignant Zareb or Zawadi's brusqueness. Although their actions upset her at the time, they had no effect on her investigation or protecting the crown prince.

Her feelings didn't matter in here. She wasn't born into a noble family, neither was she on their level.

She was the outsider, and they treated her as such, a commoner.

The next morning, Danai stood outside Prince Zawadi's apartment when he came out ready for work. He wore a ceremonial embroidered silk-mix purple tunic suit and a pair of two-toned black leather and purple suede loafers.

"Good morning, Your Highness," she greeted.

"Morning, Ms Ruga. Did you have a good night?" he responded as he walked along the airy corridor.

She nearly stumbled in surprise at his friendliness. Perhaps this was his way of apologising for yesterday's awkwardness and clearing the air.

"I had a good night. Thank you, Your Highness," she replied.

"You're welcome," he said. The rest of the walk was in silence, a comfortable silence disturbed only by the swish of fabric and thud of footsteps on the hard marble flooring.

When they got to his office, she checked it over before he got to work.

Later, the crown prince had meetings in parliament. They left the palace and travelled in a three-car convoy.

Danai sat in the same car as the prince, in the front with the driver. She coordinated movements with the security team in the other vehicles.

The meeting took most of the day, and when they returned to the palace, it was dark. Still, the prince returned to the office and worked late. When they walked back to his apartment, it was well past 9pm.

The rest of the week was filled with similar daily activities. The prince lived as *the* working royal perfectly. He woke early and worked until late every night. None of his brothers worked harder than he did, in her opinion.

The only different day was Friday.

Danai was supposed to have the day off. But she wanted to check out the prince's routine.

He rose early and spent the morning with his father before they travelled to the Regents Avenue Mosque.

Danai had to wear an abaya, a loose-fitting long-sleeved robe covering her from neck to feet, over her leggings, vest, and shoes.

Although the length of the robe could be a hindrance if she needed to move fast, she had learned to manoeuvre in the outfit. Her handgun was in a shoulder strap under the robe, and she could reach it quickly by ripping the Velcro strap at the front of the dress. Then, if she needed to run, she would gather the robe in one hand and leg it.

She'd known to pack the appropriate clothing for the required occasions, like visits to the mosque. Otherwise, she would've been excluded from the premises.

As it was, she'd had to stay in the women's section while the male guards had accompanied the prince. However, she could still observe proceedings from the mezzanine.

The prince spent a few hours there talking to the clerics. When they returned to the palace, the prince and the king had a family meal.

Danai returned to the staff quarters for her food too.

She'd sat at a table with Yusuf and some of the other guards.

"So, how do you think we're going to do this time at the match?" a male guard named Amadu asked.

"What match?" Danai asked.

"It's a rugby match between the princes and the guards. We play every quarter," Yusuf said.

"Really?" she was intrigued because one, it was rugby. She loved sports. Two, the concept of the royals playing sports with commoners was new to her. "But rugby? There are supposed to be fifteen players in a team, and there are only four princes. How does that work?"

"You know about rugby sports?" Amadu asked, eyes wide.

"Yes, I do. So how does the 'princes vs guards' thing work?"

"It's a Rugby Sevens match, so only seven players are needed on each team," Yusuf said. "Only three of the princes play regularly."

"Yes. The Quiet One doesn't play," chimed in the other guard, Pierre.

"The Quiet One? Who's that?" Danai asked, interested that they'd given the princes aliases.

Amadu laughed. "That's Prince Zediah because he was reclusive and always disappearing for months on end. I think he spent a lot of time in London, England."

"Well, he's not so quiet now that he has a heavily pregnant wife and a little boy running around the palace. That child is a handful. He gets everywhere. Have you seen him?" Pierre asked, beaming with a nostalgic smile as if he was fond of the little prince.

"Yes, I saw Prince Nour holding his father's hand as they walked towards the family dining room earlier. Princess Riona looked radiant with her baby bump. But you're right. She looks like that baby is ready to come anytime."

"She is really lovely—"

"Enough," Yusuf said in a harsh voice, interrupting Amadu. "You gossip like a woman."

Amadu frowned, looking down at the table. "I wasn't gossiping."

Obviously, Yusuf was the senior in rank to the other two as they seemed to defer to him.

"No, he wasn't." Danai reached out and patted Amadu's hand on the table. "He was just giving me information that would help me do my job better. At least I want to know if the little prince will come running around the corner in case of an emergency."

Danai made a mental note to chat one-to-one with Amadu. He would give her the low-down on the goings-on within the palace. Maybe even give her a clue as to who the mole was.

"Anyway, we were talking about Rugby," Yusuf said.

"Yes. Who are the people that make up the rest of the princes' team?" Danai asked.

"The princes recruit their friends to play to make up the numbers."

"Okay. So, who plays for the guards?"

"I'm the team captain," Yusuf said. "Then, there's Amadu, Pierre and many from the rest of the security team."

"Great. I would like to sign up for the team.," Danai said, getting excited. She loved rugby, played it in school and university. She would have loved to carry on playing. But there wasn't a structured women's league like there was in soccer.

"You. Sign up? You're a woman," Yusuf said.

"Yes, I know that." She rolled her eyes heavenwards.

"Do you know how to play?" Amadu asked.

"Yes, I'm good at it. I'm a guard. I should be able to play for the guards' team," she said, looking at Yusuf, who was frowning at her.

"We have enough players," Yusuf said.

"I don't mind being a substitute. I just want to get the chance to play rugby."

"Sorry, rugby is not a sport for women." Yusuf pushed his chair back and lifted his tray, walking away.

Danai was still trying to lift her lips off the floor at the blatant sexism. She didn't even know what to say as the other men got up and left the table too, although Amadu mouthed an apology as he went.

***

On Saturday, she got up for her morning workout. However, it was her day off, so she didn't rise as early as usual.

The palace was like a small town with different facilities onsite. A fully kitted gymnasium and sports ground featured everything one could find in a functional gym out in town. It was open to staff as well as the royals.

She had been using it daily.

However, after her five-mile run, she decided to kickbox and pound out her frustrations from the week out on the free-standing boxing bag.

Danai was pissed. Seriously, freaking pissed. It wasn't just one bad day but a whole ass bad week since arriving at the palace six days ago.

"Woah!" An amused male voice cut into her concentration.

Danai grabbed the swinging bag so it didn't hit her in the face and tilted her head. She'd been in the zone and hadn't heard anyone approach.

"Prince Azikiwe! Sorry. I didn't hear you come in." she stepped away from the bag and dropped her hands.

He was dressed in a sports kit and trainers. It looked like he'd come to work out too.

"No need to apologise," the prince grinned as he came close, palms raised. "I was just having some sympathy for the punching bag. It looked like you wanted to pound it into submission."

The prince's smile was infectious, and she couldn't help smiling back. She'd interacted with him a few times, and he had always been pleasant. Out of all the princes, he was the most easy-going. He knew how to make people feel at ease.

"It's just been a long week. I like to work out my stresses on the bag. It's better than punching someone in the face."

"Oh, I see. My brothers have been giving you a hard time."

"Actually, your brothers I can handle. It's the guards that pissed me off last night."

"Oh. What happened. I want the goss," he said, eyes twinkling.

She laughed, shaking her head.

"Oh, come on. You can tell me." He winked at her. "I'm a great listener.

"Okay. I found out about the 'princes vs guards' rugby match," she said as she walked over, picked her water bottle with the glove on and guzzled some water.

"Yes?" he said, encouraging her to continue.

"And I told Yusuf, who is the team captain, that I wanted to join the team, and he said no." She hadn't expected such a blatant rejection purely because she was a woman. She'd been hoping to use the rugby sport to bond with the guards. Instead, it seemed they didn't want her.

"He did?"

"His exact words were 'rugby is not a sport for women'."

"Well, that's as sexist as they come. But it's good."

"Good? You think his sexism is good?" Danai raged, forgetting this was a prince. What was wrong with all the men around here? She thought this one, at least, was one of the good ones.

"No. I didn't mean his words were good. I meant that him not accepting you into the guards' team is good for us. Because I can recruit you for the princes' team."

"Wait. You can't be serious." Her eyes were nearly popping from the sockets.

This was the last thing she expected. These were royals. One, she was female, as Yusuf had rudely reminded her. Two, she wasn't a princess.

"I'm serious. We're two players short, so we're desperate to make up the numbers."

"Oh. So, you want me on your team only because you're desperate." She yanked at the strap of her boxing gloves to remove it in frustration, but it didn't come off.

"No. That's not what I said." He indicated her hand. "Do you need help with that?"

"Yes. Please." She said in a disgruntled voice.

"First of all, I'm not too egotistical to admit when I'm desperate for help, and we need your help to play the match." He came closer and peeled the Velcro, sliding the glove off her palm. "Also, if you're good enough to want to play for the guards' team, then you're good enough to play for the princes' team."

"Okay." A smile tugged the corner of her lips.

He really was a charmer and knew how to melt her anger.

"So, can I add you to the team sheet?" Smiling, he took her other hand and tugged the strap of the glove.

"Yes—"

"What's going on here?"

The cold, stern voice had Danai jerking and her heart racing from recognition.

"Uh-oh. Here comes trouble," Prince Azikiwe said in a low, conspiratorial voice and winked at her as he released her hand.

Almost afraid of what she was about to face, she slowly tilted her head.

Prince Zawadi stood by the edge of the weights area.

He looked insanely hot in his sports gear, which clung to his muscular chest and thighs.

And the thunderous expression on his face indicated he was furious.

# CHAPTER NINE

Zawadi loved his brothers.

But there was no one farthest from him in personality than his immediate younger brother Azikiwe.

They were as different as fire and ice, chaos and control. Zik was the former, Zawadi the latter.

Zawadi was the eye to Azikiwe's storm.

Zawadi had never felt he needed Azikiwe's charm and wit when he had intellect and integrity.

To be fair, the differences in their personalities didn't make Zik a lousy person.

In fact, Zik was the least likely to provoke anyone. He was amiable and made friends quickly across the board. He was flexible and easily adapted to any environment he found himself in.

Yet, there was one thing about him that Zawadi always worried would land Zik into trouble one day.

His casual affairs with women.

Zawadi would never claim to be pious—he had his vices. However, compared to Zik's numerous liaisons, Zawadi was chaste.

Still, in all his various flings, Zik had never tangled with a palace employee. He understood the immorality and illegality of such an act. Employees were strictly out of bounds, and such liaisons were dishonourable.

Zik had honour. And Zawadi respected him for it.

Still, when Zawadi walked into the gymnasium this morning and saw his PPO near his brother, the two of them talking intimately and smiling at each other, only one thing came to mind.

Zik was having an illicit affair with the covert agent.

Perhaps that was why Ms Ruga had been assigned to investigate the palace leaks. Maybe she and his brother had been having an affair right when Zawadi first met the woman.

Disappointment tightened Zawadi's chest, his control vanishing. Fury took over.

His brother had no right to do this. Had no right to sully the family name in this manner.

Certainly not with Ms Ruga.

She was Zawadi's personal bodyguard. Zawadi's ... responsibility.

Not Zik's.

Zawadi had ignored Zik's excesses in the past. But he wouldn't overlook this one.

He couldn't. He couldn't allow his brother to treat her in the same casual manner he treated all the other women, discarding them afterwards like expired goods.

Not to mention this felt like ... betrayal. His lungs constricted, making it hard to breathe.

"What's going on here?" He barely stopped himself from stomping over there and yanking the two of them apart.

They jolted apart like two lovers who had been caught in flagrante delicto. More proof that there was something improper going on.

Ms Ruga was barely clothed in the pair of stretchy gym shorts and a tank top that moulded her glistening sweaty toned body. Her braids were pulled away from her face and tied into a bunch at the nape.

Zik was no more covered in his running shorts and t-shirt combo.

They were not naked. But anyone could have walked in on them.

"Bro, I can explain," Zik said as he walked up to Zawadi, grinning.

The smile on his brother's face only wound Zawadi up. How could Zik be so blasé about something so unethical?

"Explain what?" Zawadi's voice dripped with disapproval. "That you're having an affair with my bodyguard."

Ms Ruga spat out a mouthful of water she'd just sipped.

"Woah!" Zik exclaimed, jerking back with a bemused expression. "Where did you get that idea?"

"Your intimate proximity with each other a few minutes ago." His gaze bounced between the two of them, uncertainty niggling at him. Did he get it wrong?

"I have no interest whatsoever in Prince Zik." Danai dabbed her face with a towel, the other hand on her hip as she glared at Zawadi. "No offence, Your Highness."

"None taken, Danai." Zik narrowed his eyes and crossed his arms over his chest. "Let me spell it out for you, bro. I don't want to have sex with your PPO."

Zawadi grimaced at Zik's directness.

"I know you think I'm a man-whore," Zik continued. "But I've never touched an employee. I'm not about to start now."

Okay. Zik's sharp tone meant that Zawadi had offended him. Zik was not easily offended. He was the sunshine one compared to his siblings, always cheerful.

Zawadi's cheeks heated that he'd drawn the wrong conclusion. "I saw the two of you being cosy and assumed something more was going on."

"Yes, you made the wrong assumptions. I can talk to a woman without wanting to get into her knickers." Zik didn't seem ready to let it go.

Zawadi sighed. "Okay. I get it. I was wrong."

"Yes, you were." He rolled his eyes and shook his head. "Anyway, Danai and I were talking about next month's rugby match. I asked her to join the princes' team, and she said yes."

"You did what?" It was Zawadi's turn to cross his arms over his chest as his gaze flicked from Zik to an annoyed-looking Danai and back.

The Princes vs Guards Rugby Sevens tournament was Zawadi's brainchild.

As a prince, he couldn't play regular competitive rugby or join a team in the national league because of national security and wellbeing issues. Then, after his father's heart attack, when he took on more responsibilities to allow his parent to semi-retire, he had even less time for the sports he loved.

And he missed playing rugby too much to discard the activity totally. To stay active in the sports he loved, he'd set up an annual regional tournament involving grass-root community teams competing for a trophy. It was a big occasion on the local calendar. It had since spawned the international charity event of Bagumi vs The Rest of the World.

The upcoming match was a 'friendly' precursor for the main event in about six months.

"Remember you asked me to recruit for the team," Zik said and swivelled to indicate Danai with both hands. "She was available because the guards decided they didn't want her."

Zawadi shook his head in exasperation. "Did you stop to think that maybe the guards didn't want her in the team because she doesn't know how to play?"

"Of course, she knows how to play." The now smiling Zik flicked his gaze back to the silent covert agent. "Danai, what position do you usually play?"

Zawadi scratched his chin. "You mean you didn't know what position she played, and you asked her to join us?"

Zik didn't seem fazed, as if he already had everything covered. "I was going to ask her. I barely convinced her to join us before you barged in and accused us of having an affair."

Zawadi grimaced at the reminder of his blunder. Then he turned to Danai. "Ms Ruga, what position do you play?"

She eyeballed him, her mouth set in a grim line for a few heart-thumping seconds in silence.

His gaze drifted to her lips. She wore no makeup, and her lips were nude-brown, full, and oval-shaped, tapering at the corners. Would they be soft to the touch, sweet to taste—

"I'm not going to tell you until I get an apology from you for accusing me of having an affair with your brother."

Ms Ruga's sharp, contemptuous tone cut into his daydream.

"What?" Zawadi frowned, trying to get his bearing while mentally kicking himself.

What was with him lately? He'd thought his rambling thoughts were being overwhelmed by the assassination attempt. The week had gone in a haze of activity. But there were quiet moments when thoughts of his new bodyguard crept into his subconscious.

"In fact, I'm not going to play for the princes' team without an apology from you," Ms Ruga said. "And as I see it, you guys will have to concede the match as a loss if you don't field enough players."

Grabbing her towel and bottle, she walked towards the far side of the gym with yoga mats on the floor.

Zawadi stood there, gobsmacked that she'd walked away from him without his dismissal.

First, it was rude. In the past, people had been convicted of treason for less.

Secondly, no one had ever done that to him before. No one should do it to the crown prince of Bagumi and get away with it.

Yet, he wasn't even sure what to do about it.

Strangely, something sizzled in his vein. Something he couldn't quite name.

His brother rounded on him, cutting away the view of Ms Ruga. "You better go and apologise to her."

"What? No. Didn't you see what she just did?"

"You mean because she walked away from you?"

"Yes. No one has ever done that to me before."

"Well, suck it up, bro. Unless you want to arrest her for treason." Zik sounded amused.

Zawadi stiffened. The thought of Ms Ruga in jail didn't sit well with him. "It's not funny."

"No, it's not. We can't afford to lose the next match. So don't mess this up," Zik said.

His brother was right. None of the princes liked losing a match. They were highly competitive and fought hard to win all their games. So, losing this one purely because of his ego would be stupid.

"But how do you know she will be any good at the sport?" Zawadi asked, still eyeing Danai, who was lying on a mat, doing stomach crunches.

"Because any woman who volunteers to participate in a mainly male team is gutsy and strong. You already know she can hold her own. She works in a male-dominated field as it is. I want her in my team, not playing against us."

"Zik is right," Zareb's voice came from behind Zawadi.

Zawadi shook his head. Not him as well. "How long have you been there?"

"Long enough to tell you that you should go and apologise to Ms Ruga so she can play for our team," Zareb said.

"Hmmm?" Zawadi tilted back to look at his youngest brother. "I thought you didn't like her."

Zareb lifted his shoulders in a shrug. "I don't like her interfering in my operations. But I know that she's an excellent rugby player. She played Varsity Rugby, and her team took the trophy home for the three seasons she played before graduation. She is a great finisher. She can play in the winger position."

"How do you know this?" Zawadi's face puckered in a frown.

"I read her file," Zareb said.

Now, there was something Zawadi could do. Read Ms Ruga's dossier to find out more about her. What kind of person she was, her goals and aspirations…?

What are you doing?

Zawadi shook his head, clearing his thoughts.

"Go on, then." Zik nudged his shoulder. "You asked me to recruit the team. Don't sabotage me. I swear if you don't go and apologise to her now, I'm not going to play the next match."

Damn. His brother was playing hardball. No way they wouldn't struggle at the match without Zik as a playmaker. Great with the fancy creative stuff, he was nifty with his hands as a catcher, agile, a strong defender and an excellent tactical runner. Depending on the squad, he could alternate between the flyhalf position and the centre position.

Zareb was a scrumhalf while Zawadi played in the hooker position. They needed Zik.

"Fine," Zawadi said, conceding he didn't have much choice.

He strode to where Ms Ruga stood, stretching her muscles, and stopped behind her. He kept his gaze averted so he didn't have to stare at the damp clothes clinging to her body. He swallowed and cleared his throat.

"Ms Ruga, may I have your attention for a moment," he said.

"I'm listening," she said but didn't turn around.

His spine stiffened at her rebuff, and annoyance rose within him. She was rude again.

"Turn around," he commanded in a sharp tone.

"No. This is my day off. You don't have the right to order me to do anything today." She carried on with her stretches, ignoring him.

Damn. Her stubbornness was both alluring and annoying at the same time.

He puffed out a sigh. She was right, though. This was her personal time.

And he needed her more than she needed him right now.

"I'm sorry for accusing you falsely," he said in a calm tone, hoping to pacify her. "I hope you will accept our invitation to join our rugby sevens' team. If you wish to be part of the team, be out on the sports field in thirty minutes for today's training session."

He wouldn't beg. The ball was in her court now. He swivelled, ready to walk away.

"Thirty minutes!" She jerked around, facing him. "I've just had a workout. I need to rest."

Now, he had her attention. She looked flustered for the first time today.

Playing hardball, too, he could barely hide the amusement curling one corner of his lips.

"I'm the captain," he said without amusement. "If you want to be part of my team, you will train with the team. So be out there in thirty minutes."

Her mouth hung open in a shocked expression as he turned and walked away.

His brothers barely contained their chuckles.

"You two better be out there in thirty minutes as well. There will be no slackers in my team," he said to them as he left the gymnasium, their laughter ringing behind him.

A smile broke on his lips when he stepped into the sunshine. Excitement fluttered in his gut too.

It would be an interesting training day.

# CHAPTER TEN

*Damn, he's hot.*

The thought ran through Danai's mind while Crown Prince Zawadi dictated his expectations from her as part of the princes' rugby team. He'd already apologised for accusing her of sleeping with his brother.

Weird. Her initial anger at his false accusation had faded, replaced by this warmth in her belly as she stared at his rugged facial features and deep black eyes.

She could use other words to describe him, but her brain cells only seemed interested in one right now.

Hot.

He filled out the two-tone, funnel neck, long-sleeved black and grey tracksuit covering him from collar to ankles. His trainers were black with white soles, similar to what she had on.

She'd never seen him in any attire that bared his skin apart from hands and face. All his tunics and dress-shirts were long-sleeved, and of course, he always wore trousers.

It was the mix of intense intelligence and athleticism about him that drew her attention. He wasn't the arrogant sports star who walked around with a smirk like Prince Zareb. Or even the sexy heartbreaker always photographed with women hanging off his arms like Prince Zik. Neither was he the reclusive new-age artiste like Prince Zediah.

He was Prince Zawadi, unique and owning her at this moment, considering he'd managed to flip the situation around to have her on the defensive.

Before she could tell him that she needed at least an hour to eat a meal and recoup her strength, he was already striding away from her to the gym exit.

Prince Zik sauntered over, still chuckling. "He's something else, isn't he?"

"You can say that again," Danai muttered as she packed up her kit. "I need food and a shower. I don't have enough time."

"You're going to be training with a bunch of sweaty men." The prince grinned. "None of us will mind if you're already sweaty. But I get it. It's a woman thing. So go grab a quick shower in the locker room, and I'll order you a protein shake from the gym café."

"Oh, sure. That will be great." She grabbed her bag, ready for the bathroom.

"What's your boot size? I'm thinking about eight?" Prince Zik asked, looking at her trainers as he pulled a phone from his pocket.

She paused. "Eight and a half. Why?"

"Those indoor trainers won't help on the field. You need studded boots. I'm responsible for making sure everyone has the right kit. I should have something ready by the time you finish in the shower."

"Am I getting a jersey as well?" she asked.

"Sure."

"And you know my size?"

"Of course." He winked and turned away to speak to someone on the phone.

The prince really lived up to his reputation. He must order female clothing frequently to be able to assess her size by just looking at her.

Shaking her head, she hurried towards the changing rooms and past Prince Zareb, who had climbed onto a rowing machine. "Good morning, Your Highness."

"Good morning," he replied with a nod.

In the female changing room, she stripped down, wrapped her hair into a top bun to avoid getting it wet and walked into one of the cubicles. The warm water from the showerhead helped loosen her muscles, and the pinpricks on her skin shook off the tiredness.

She soaped her body, rinsed off and was out ten minutes later. She didn't bother creaming her body, only her face and some Vaseline on her elbows and knees. No time for anything else except for deodorant. Anyway, she would need another shower after the training session. Hopefully, it would only last a couple of hours.

She tugged on a t-shirt and pulled on the shorts she'd worn earlier, praying the outfit wasn't stinky.

A knock sounded on the locker room door.

"Danai, it's Zik. I brought your kit." He spoke from outside the closed door.

She hurried over and tugged the door open.

Sure enough, he stood there with a package in his hands.

"How?" She looked up at him.

"The sports apparel shop at the bottom of Regents Avenue couriered it over. They always stock our kits in case of an emergency. One of the perks of being royals." He shoved the parcel at her.

"Thank you." She shut the door and returned to the bench to change again. Everything fit, even the boots. Then she stowed her bag in a locker and went back to the gymnasium.

Prince Zik waited for her at the café. "Your protein shake. Drink up."

She wasn't a big fan of milkshakes, but there wasn't another option with less than ten minutes to get some nutrients into her body. So, it was either a milkshake or a smoothie.

"Come on," he said when she gulped the last drop. "We don't want to be late."

She grabbed her water bottle and followed him, and they hurried out towards the playing fields.

***

Three hours later, Danai was beginning to wish she hadn't said yes to Zik's request to join their team.

Zawadi Saene was a taskmaster. Damn.

They had been in physical training for the past three hours with only short breaks in between. He hadn't even considered that she was a woman and should expend less effort than the men. Instead, he'd made her do exactly everything the rest of the eleven men in the team did. Aside from the initial expressions of shock by the others, they'd all soon ignored her presence as a female and treated her the same as anyone else.

She had sworn not to complain even one bit. She didn't want to come across as weak or incapable.

It wasn't as if she hadn't done similar things in the past.

The training was as rigorous as the one she had to do before she joined military intelligence. But in the years since, she hadn't undergone anything as strenuous as this. So, her body was feeling the impact.

Now she sat on a chair in the gym café, eating lunch. She was hungry, but she could barely hold cutlery.

They had two hours break before the evening training session.

She wanted to go back to her studio and sleep. But she was afraid she wouldn't get up in time for the afternoon session. Also, she didn't want to give the impression that she wasn't as good as the men.

The team had taken over the gym restaurant for lunch. The staff had joined several small tables to make one long wooden table, which the group sat around.

The men were made up of the princes' friends. Most notably, Ejike and Ekene Onoh were Nigerian princes and brothers to Prince Zawadi's fiancée. She'd been surprised when they'd disembarked the helicopter which had landed on the palace lawn earlier. They had travelled from Nigeria just for the training session. Even her colleague, Razi Hamadou, from the BIS, was here.

Amazing how many people went out of their way to participate in this event. Went to show the influence Prince Zawadi and his siblings wielded.

Razi, who was sitting next to her, pushed away from the table. "I have to go. I have some errands to run."

"Okay. See you later," Danai said.

Most of the others left once they finished their meals. However, Prince Zareb hadn't joined them. Instead, he'd gone straight to the house he shared with his fiancée Malika, which was outside the palace grounds.

Eventually, Prince Zik left with the Onoh brothers, leaving only her and Prince Zawadi.

The crown prince got up from his seat and walked over. He pulled out the chair opposite hers and settled on it, placing elbows against the table.

"How do you feel?" he asked in a concerned voice, brows wrinkled. "Are you hurting?"

His dark eyes examined her face, scanned her body as if checking for injuries.

Her skin tingled, her heartbeat racing. She touched her throat, unable to hide the surprise. One, he'd come over, and two, he sounded worried about her.

Memories from their daily routines played back. He always enquired if she'd had a good night every morning. She'd assumed he was polite. Perhaps he truly cared about her wellbeing. The same way he cared about everyone else around him.

The contrast between the domineering man, who owned the world and seemed to expect everyone to toe the line, and the compassionate man who looked at her as if he genuinely cared disarmed her. How could she fight him when he was considerate?

"Not hurting. Just tired. I could use a nap," she said—no need pretending otherwise.

"Then go and take a nap," he said quietly, his tone reassuring.

She sighed. "I can't. If I do, I won't wake in time for the afternoon session."

"Take a nap. It's an order," he said in a stern voice.

She jerked upright, glaring at him as her spine stiffened.

A smile curled the corner of his lips as if he'd expected her to push against his order. "I'll set a wake-up call for you. Go on. You'll thank me later."

"Yeah, right." She gave him a wry smile. "I'll thank you if you let me skip the afternoon session instead."

He chuckled, the sound rich and surprising, sending a rush of warmth across her chest.

"No," his voice rumbled. "If I let you skip the session, you'll accuse me of treating you differently because you're a woman. And that would be sexism. We can't have that, Ms Ruga."

Speechless, she stared at him for a few seconds. He had her there. She wouldn't appreciate any special concessions on her account. If she didn't know better, she would think the man was studying her and learning about her because he was interested in her.

Just in her imagination, though. First, because she wasn't a princess and two, he was already betrothed to a real-life one and would be wedding the woman soon.

She shoved back the chair and stood. "I'll see you later, Your Highness."

"Of course, you will, Ms Ruga." There was still humour in his voice.

Another rush of warmth surprised her. This man was different from the standoffish, autocratic prince she'd encounter the day she arrived at the palace. She'd since discovered him to be humorous and compassionate. While he didn't have Zik's charm, he was more approachable than first impressions suggested.

As she walked away, her nape prickled with heat. Her pulse raced, and she was suddenly alert as her senses heightened.

Was he watching her?

Nah. It couldn't be. The crown prince of the Kingdom of Bagumi couldn't be staring at her commoner behind.

But when she reached the door, she glanced towards the table.

Sure enough, Prince Zawadi was staring at her.

She pushed the swinging door, stepped into the sunshine, and clutched her chest. "Be still, my beating heart."

# CHAPTER ELEVEN

The Saturday afternoon nap did the trick. Zawadi kept his promise, and Danai was awakened by a phone call. Then, feeling refreshed, the evening training session went a lot smoother.

The session ended earlier than she'd anticipated. She'd thought they would be there for three hours. However, they only spent ninety minutes. She had about thirty minutes with the physiotherapist. By the time she showered, changed, and took the long walk back to the staff quarters, the princes were nowhere to the found.

Even the staff communal areas seemed to be deserted.

Where was everyone?

She went to her studio, dumped her gym bag, and went back outside. She took a stroll through the summer garden, past the Crown office towards the royal residences.

Palace employees stood outside the building as if awaiting an arrival.

A black SUV came up the long drive and stopped in front of the tiered entrance to the palace. Servants stepped down and opened the back doors as others went to the boot and started dislodging the luggage.

Prince Zareb came out from one side, and a young woman came out from the other.

Danai recognised her from photographs.

Princess Amira, the youngest of the Saene siblings, was home. She'd probably flown from the United States where she lived with her husband to visit for Prince Zediah's baby shower happening tomorrow.

The news was that she'd met her husband online, a thoroughly modern marriage, considering Bagumi was a conservative country in many aspects.

Zareb was smiling and chatting with his sister as they entered the building.

Danai had never seen the prince smile that much since she'd been working here. He obviously held affection for his youngest sibling.

She expected the other Saene princesses would return home too for the baby shower—Princess India from the Kingdom of Sudar, where her husband was the king and Princess Isha from Wanai, where her husband was the president.

Anyway, none of that was her headache tonight.

Still, she put in a call to the security suite to be notified if the crown prince planned to leave the palace during the night. Afterwards, she returned to her studio and pigged out in front of the TV before crawling into bed.

The next day it was back to business as usual, and Danai was back on PPO duty.

She stopped over at the security suite for a briefing from the team leader, Harry. It had been a quiet night. However, there were heavy activities on the monitors. Delivery vans arriving with party decorations and catering equipment. Palace staff bustled as they prepared for the upcoming event.

Today was the baby shower party for Prince Zediah's and Princess Riona's unborn child.

"Just a heads up. Princess Amara Onoh is visiting today," Harry said.

Danai's heart slammed in her chest. She recognised the name. That was Prince Zawadi's betrothed.

She made sure her facial expression didn't change and said, "I suppose she is a party guest."

"She is, but you know she is also the crown prince's fiancée. Her entourage has requested that Prince Zawadi not be informed of her arrival. She wants to surprise him."

Danai huffed. She wasn't paid to keep secrets for the woman. Moreover, this was a security risk.

"Who are the people on her entourage? Have we screened them?" she asked.

Harry typed on the keyboard, and dossiers appeared on the monitor in front of him. "Here is the file the Nigerians sent us. She has a personal bodyguard and an assistant. The bodyguard, Reggie, has been with her for years. The assistant is new."

Danai flicked through the dossiers. Nothing stood out. But the niggle on her spine persisted. "Did we run our own checks on these people?"

"Well, no." He frowned. "They are the princess's entourage. Not our headache."

"It is our headache when two unverified people will be spending the night in the palace."

"But the file came from the Nigerian Security Services."

"I wouldn't trust the Nigerian Security Services to find their grandmas in a room full of old women. Do you not see the security nightmare going on in that country? How they've let BH terrorists and other banditry run rampant. Every day people are being massacred or kidnapped. Hang on, have you forgotten that our Princess Isha went missing from Lagos almost two years ago? Thankfully, no harm came to her. But don't you see how bad things could have gotten?"

Harry nodded. "You're right. I'm sorry. I will forward their details to BIS for verification."

"Do that straight away. I need printed copies. Does Prince Zareb know the situation?"

"Not yet. He's been distracted by the arrival of his sisters. Princess Amira came home last night, and Princesses India and Isha are arriving this morning."

"Okay. I'll speak to him. Also, send a message to the front gates to do an extra sweep on the car when it arrives. I want the bags and bodies screened. Use the dogs as well. And the bodyguard should be disarmed. He shouldn't have any weaponry when he enters the palace."

"They are not going to like it," Harry said.

"I don't care." She grabbed the printouts and headed for the door.

"By the way, I heard you joined the princes' rugby team," he said.

"Yes. What about it?" she turned in his direction with a frown.

"Nothing. Just that you chose the wrong side."

"I chose? I never chose anything. Yusuf said I couldn't join the guards' team, and the princes' invited me to join theirs."

"That's not what I heard."

Danai's back stiffened. The staff were gossiping about her and obviously not telling the truth.

"I don't care what you heard. You should stop listening to gossip. Anyway, thanks for this, Harry."

"You're welcome," he called out as she left the suite and walked towards Zareb's office.

She was knocking on the door as he sauntered into the lobby.

"Ms Ruga, you were looking for me?" he asked as he pulled out his keys and opened the door.

"Yes. I need to talk to you about this." She dropped the file on his desk. "We have unverified visitors arriving today."

With a frown on his face, he settled in the armchair and lifted the folder. He took out the photo at the top. "We already screened and cleared the bodyguard when he started visiting with the princess a few years ago." He tossed the picture on the table and lifted the next one. "She is new. We cleared her last assistant but not this one."

He lifted the phone on the table straight away, pressed a button, and waited a few seconds before speaking. "Why wasn't I notified about the change in Princess Amara's entourage ... Contact BIS about screening the assistant ... Good."

He hung up. "You asked for BIS to screen the bodyguard too?"

"Yes, I did," Danai said. "Since he's been to the palace several times before, he is a suspect in the assassination attempt since we still don't know the co-conspirators. He's had access to the prince's office and residence and could have easily relayed the information. Right now, everyone is a suspect until they are eliminated."

"You're correct. We can't rule out anyone until we're sure. We're going to need to do body screens and disarm the bodyguard when they arrive."

"Yes, I already gave the instructions to the team for a frisk search and baggage scans."

He nodded. "Good. Although the princess isn't going to be happy about that. Do you want me to be there?"

"No. I can take the heat." It was nice of him to offer, but she was getting used to dealing with obnoxious royals. One more would not hurt.

"Good." He put the printout back in the file. "I was going to have you assigned to the baby shower. Thought you might like the entertainment."

"Hell, no!" she said in reflex. The last place she wanted to be was around women 'oohing' and 'aahing' over babies.

He jerked as if stunned by her outburst.

"Unless Prince Zawadi is going to be there," she added for clarification. He was her priority.

"No. It's a women-only party," he said.

"Then, no. I will be with the crown prince, which reminds me, I need to head down there." She glanced at her watch. It was ten past eight o'clock.

"You can go. I saw him headed to the library," Prince Zareb said.

"Thank you," Danai said and hurried out of his office, across the lobby and through the courtyard to a separate building, which housed the palace library and museum.

There were hand-drawn portraits of every Bagumian king from the 18th century until now hanging on the walls of the spacious gallery. Also, artefacts, sculptures, weavings, mats, attires, and tools their ancestors used.

She walked through another turnstile and security point into the library—wall-to-floor-to-ceiling dark shelves filled with books. The place was awe-inspiring, and she felt as if she should tiptoe so as not to make any noise.

She found Prince Zawadi in an alcove, sitting in a low leather armchair, glasses perched on his nose and a leather-bound book in his hand. He wore a midi-length teal tunic over matching trousers and black velvet loafers with teal monograms.

Her heart stuttered.

He was giving off the hot nerd vibe, and she was a goner.

What she wouldn't give to have him moan her name even once. But that was never going to happen. She really had to get a grip.

She would find a fuckboy at the earliest opportunity, book a hotel room, and satisfy every craving she'd had since she started working at the palace.

Because she had to stamp out this craving she had for the crown prince that would only lead to trouble. She couldn't have him, and he probably saw her as an annoying nuisance he would like to dispose.

She walked up to Amadu, who stood a few feet away from the prince behind a bookshelf.

"You can take a break. I'll take over," she said in a low voice.

"Okay." Amadu turned and walked away.

She approached Prince Zawadi. "Good morning, Your Highness."

He looked up, pushing the spectacles up the bridge of his nose. "Good morning, Ms Ruga. How are you feeling today?"

"I'm good, sir. The session with the physio last night helped a lot."

"Oh, good. I'm glad." He placed a handcrafted bookmark between the pages and closed the book. "I asked Zareb to assign you to the baby shower today so you can get a little downtime and not be on your feet all day."

So, he'd been the one who had requested the reassignment because he was concerned she would be exhausted from the training.

Damn. He was a compassionate man. Warmth bloomed in her chest. How could she not fall for him?

She swallowed to clear the lump in her throat. "Thank you, Your Highness. But there's no need. I'd rather be here."

His lips twitched as he leaned into the chair. He looked like he was suppressing laughter, although his eyes twinkled. "You mean, you're scared of talking babies all day."

"I'm not scared of anything," she replied a little too quick.

He raised a brow as if he didn't believe her. He'd figured her out. How?

She sighed. "You're right. I'm not very maternal. Babies are not for me."

His forehead wrinkled. He stared at her with piercing onyx eyes. "Are you saying you're not interested in being a mother someday?"

She shook out her shoulder, hands clasped in front. She'd been asked variations of this question before. Somehow everyone expected her to want children because she was a woman.

"I don't believe every woman is meant to be a mother. And I'm one of those. I think I would probably make any children I had miserable."

"I don't believe that." He shook his head.

"Think about it. I'd spend most of the time away from them working because I won't give up my job. Then when I'm with them, I'd probably smother them by being too overprotective. They'll hate me."

"I see what you mean," he said with a contemplative expression. "So, you see yourself working for the BIS until you retire."

"Pretty much. Otherwise, I would work for a different law enforcement service like the police in the CID."

"Good to know." He picked up his book again. "Since you're avoiding babies. May I suggest you join me in reading a book. Just select whatever you want to read, grab a seat and enjoy."

"Sure, Thank you, Your Highness." She shifted. "But there's something I need to tell you first."

"Oh." He put the book down. "Go on."

"We received a message that Princess Amara is visiting the palace today."

"She is?" He grabbed his phone from the table. "I don't have a message from her."

"That's probably because she wanted it to be a surprise for you."

"Is that so?" He leaned into the chair with a frown. "So why are you telling me?"

She rubbed a hand over her brow. "Unfortunately, there is a security issue. Someone in her entourage is not cleared by the BIS, and the other needs his clearance reviewed because of the assassination attempt."

"But her people should have cleared her staff already."

"Yes, I know. But we're extra-cautious. Until we clear them, they can't have direct access to you. So, we're going to restrict their movements to the guest suite while the princess is here. I wanted to inform you before the princess arrives so it doesn't come as a shock."

He didn't say anything for a little while and then nodded. "Thank you, Ms Ruga."

"You're welcome, Your Highness." She stepped back and went in search of a book to read, relieved that he'd taken it so well.

She had a feeling Princess Amara would not be so accommodating.

# CHAPTER TWELVE

"BCC just arrived at the gates," Harry said in the earpiece attached to Danai's headset.

BCC stood for Black-Crowned Crane, which was the codename for Princess Amara. It was the Nigerian National Bird, and she was a Nigerian princess. Hey, presto!

"Thanks, Harry," Danai said into the mouthpiece. She stood from the chair, which was a couple of sections away from the crown prince.

"Stay with His Highness," she said in a low voice to Amadu and hurried out of the library. She had ten minutes to get to the security lobby at the palace entrance before the car came up the long drive to the private residence.

The crown prince had been reading for a couple of hours. For someone who had been told his fiancée was going to surprise him with a visit, he didn't seem perturbed.

If it had been her that was expecting a visitor, she would have rushed home to tidy up and make sure she was wearing her best sexy lingerie.

Then again, when one was the crown prince, one didn't need sexy underwear to make a good impression. And his apartment would be cleaned by staff anyway.

It seemed the library was his place of solace. He was determined not to have the time spent there cut short earlier than necessary.

She couldn't blame him. The prince had a busy life. So, the quiet moments were rare. Considering he'd spent yesterday in the physical exhaustion of rugby training, he deserved the quiet reading time away from the rest of the palace buzzing with activities.

That fact hit her as soon as she stepped outside and took the shortcut through the gardens to get to the security lobby.

She went past the ballroom, festooned in decorations while the party planner finalised the flower arrangement.

Danai had to admit everything looked beautiful and tasteful. And expensive.

Maybe she would chance a peek towards the end of the event. Hopefully, the toddlers would be exhausted and asleep by then.

She arrived at the security lobby as the car pulled up.

A man stepped out of the front passenger seat and opened the back door.

Danai recognised him from the dossier as Princess Amara's bodyguard. A woman stepped from the other side of the car. That was the assistant.

Then Princess Amara stepped out of the car, and Danai had to admit that photographs didn't convey her beauty enough.

She was stunning. She was the epitome of a modern African princess. Dressed in red-black-gold-white, multi-geometric-print, off-the-shoulders, full-length Samakaka fabric dress with a fitted bodice and A-line skirt.

Her long glossy dark hair cascaded over her shoulder in waves, styled to perfection. Her made-up face was flawless and beautiful, although almost half of it was covered by the giant round sunshades. The jewellery on the graduated V-necklace caught the light and glittered. They were clustered diamonds set in platinum. Her earrings were pear-shaped diamonds, matching the necklace. Her manicured red vanished feet were in designer black leather stiletto sandals.

She bunched the hem of her dress and headed up the steps, hips swaying. She walked with the self-assurance only the super privileged and beautiful could attain. The princes had the same swagger.

They didn't know doubt or the fight for survival. Since birth, they had been given everything. No one refused them anything. They had power and sway very few could comprehend.

Sure, they had personal battles, and they all worked hard, Prince Zawadi especially. But they were enclosed in a bubble of utmost freedom.

Princess Amara looked every bit the princess shown on TV and the media. Faultless, proper, gentle, polished. Adjectives that could never describe Danai.

The press loved her, and she was a queen on social media with over a million followers on Twitter and Instagram.

Danai approached when she reached the lobby. "Welcome, Princess Amara. I'm Danai, Prince Zawadi's head of security."

She lifted her chin and said, "hello."

"I'm responsible for clearing you and your team this morning before you can enter the palace. Unfortunately, due to the heightened security threat, we are screening every visitor."

She tugged her glasses off, revealing startling hazel eyes. "I'm not a visitor. I'm Zawadi's fiancée."

Danai should mention she wasn't married to Zawadi yet, so she wasn't a family member. But she chose to be diplomatic as the bad news would only get worse.

"I understand, ma'am. But the prince was nearly killed recently, and I'm sure you would like us to stop it from happening again."

Princess Amara's mouth dropped open and closed. "Get on with it, then."

"This way," Danai directed her towards the body scanning arch. "Please put your phone, glasses and purse on the tray."

The princess placed her items into the plastic tray, which rolled along the conveyor belt through the X-Ray scanner.

"Please step into the body scanner, raise your hands and wait for the machine to beep."

The princess huffed but did as she was instructed. When the machine beeped, Danai indicated for her to come through. She grabbed a wand and waved it over the princess's body.

"Unfortunately, due to the short notice of your visit, your team wasn't cleared by our security agency, so they are going to be confined to your guest quarters for the duration of this trip."

"What? This is ridiculous." The princess snapped as she grabbed her items from the tray that had gone through the X-Ray machine.

"It is the new protocol. Also, your bodyguard must relinquish his weapons. He can recover them when you leave."

"This is utter nonsense. Does Zawadi know about this? I want to talk to him right away."

"Of course. I can take you to him." Danai turned to the lead security officer. "Continue with the scanner and frisk search. Once that's done, escort the visitors to the princess's guest suite."

Then she turned to Princess Amara. "This way, Your Highness."

Danai led the way. The princess's shoes clip-clopped on the marble floor, then across the cobbled stones of the courtyard into the echoing gallery, then the quiet library.

Neither said a word until Prince Zawadi came into view.

The prince looked up as they approached and stood, a smile spreading on his face. "Amara, it's so good to see you."

Amara went past Danai and clasped Prince Zawadi's arms, looking up at him.

"Darling, you don't look surprised to see me. I suppose they told you." She turned around and glared at Danai.

Danai didn't flinch. She clenched her hands behind her back and stood feet apart.

"Don't be angry. They had to tell me because of a security issue." Zawadi pressed a tender kiss to Amara's forehead.

Something wrenched in Danai's gut. She should turn away and give them a private moment. But she couldn't. She was on duty. Watching him was her job.

You just don't want to leave him alone with another woman. Admit it.

The knot in her gut tightened again. She averted her gaze. She was better than this. Stronger than this. When she got a moment, she would look through her contacts and find someone local to hook up with tonight.

The royal couple settled into two separate armchairs. Sure, they weren't the most tactile pair, and the kiss to the forehead was very chaste. Still, Zawadi cared for Amara. Otherwise, he could've lied to her and pretended that he was surprised at her presence.

"What's going on around here? The security team says my staff will be on lockdown until we leave. This is not acceptable, darling," Princess Amara's word cut into Danai's thoughts, and she stiffened.

"I know. Because of the short notice, there wasn't enough time to clear your entourage for the visit. But I will speak to Zareb about fast-tracking the verification," Prince Zawadi said in a placating tone.

"Would you, darling. That would be wonderful."

"It's not a problem."

"You didn't tell me you had a female bodyguard." The princess glanced in Danai's direction.

Prince Zawadi met Danai's gaze, but his expression was unreadable. Her heart skipped a beat. How would he explain this? She understood why the princess would be curious about her presence.

The prince turned back to his fiancée. "I didn't know you took an interest in my bodyguards."

"I don't, but she's female."

"And it matters if she's female?"

"Not if you don't think so."

"I don't. How long are you staying?

Suppressing a smile, Danai stepped further away, joining Amadu, who stood at the end of a long bookshelf, giving the royal couple space to talk or get intimate.

Prince Zawadi was a decent human being. He'd handled the complaint about the new security protocols and about Danai better than she'd expected. With consideration and integrity.

New respect for him made warmth spread through her chest.

Although Zawadi had been antagonistic when she'd first arrived, he seemed to have accepted her role as his bodyguard regardless of her gender. Just as he'd taken her playing in the princes' rugby squad despite being a woman.

He reminded her of Dad—a man who stood up for a woman's right to be non-conformist regarding traditional gender roles and expectations.

In a conservative country like Bagumi, those men were rare. And part of the reason she'd never settled down with anyone. Because finding a life partner who understood that she didn't want to live in a pre-defined box was nearly impossible.

Crown Prince Zawadi was one. Still, no matter how much Danai liked him, he was already taken.

Determination tightened Danai's muscles. She would repay his trust, not by pining for him. But by finding the mole in the palace and ensuring no harm came to him.

This was her job and should be her sole focus. Nothing else.

"Danai," the deep rumbling sound of her name sent a sizzle down her spine as she glanced at the prince.

He waved his right hand, indicating for her to come close.

She walked over to him and dipped her head. "Your Highness."

"Until my fiancée's team is given access to the palace again, you will be her personal bodyguard," the prince said, leaning into his chair.

"Oh ..." Danai stuttered as her breath hitched in shock. Refusal danced on the tip of her tongue because her assignment was the prince, not his fiancée. But she bit down the rebuttal.

Sure. Guarding the Nigerian princess wasn't on her job description, and she could challenge the order.

Still, could she deny the prince's command when he'd defended her just moments ago to said fiancée? And a rebuff would make him antagonistic, which could make her job more difficult.

"Of course, Your Highness," she replied instead.

"Good." He straightened from the chair, extending his hand to the princess. "Enjoy the party. I'll see you later."

Fabric rustled as the princess placed her palm in his and stood. "Will do, darling."

He pressed a kiss to her forehead like he'd done when she arrived.

Danai averted her gaze, and Princess Amara swept past her in a flurry of expensive fabric and plume of delicate fragrance.

She glanced at the crown prince, and he seemed to be watching them with an inscrutable expression.

"Your Highness." Danai bowed and followed the princess out of the quiet library, across the marbled floor of the royal museum into the private gardens.

Princess Amara didn't hesitate or ask for directions. She seemed to know exactly where she was going as if she was thoroughly familiar with the entire palace.

Danai had been here a few weeks and still struggled to navigate the complex buildings and corridors.

So how did a princess who only visited Darusa Palace occasionally know her way around? Prince Zawadi and Princess Amara had only been linked romantically a few months ago. Considering the woman lived in Nigeria, she could hardly visit the palace frequently in the interim.

The sound of music and merriment floated out as they neared the acre of lawn recently converted into a children's fun park. There were carousels, climbing frames, slides, a multicoloured-ball pit, a bouncy castle and even a miniature powered go-kart track.

Toddlers and pre-teens hustled from one play equipment to the next, their voices filled with excitement and laughter as what seemed like an army of nannies hovered around them.

Princess Amara didn't stop, and they walked past the huge white marquee decorated in pink, gold, and blue balloons, which had tiny, coloured tables and chairs and an entertainment stage at the end for the little people.

The princess walked through the open double doors into the palace banquet hall decorated with flowers and brocade. Women in various luxurious outfits from silk abayas and hijabs to cashmere pantsuits and chiffon cocktail dresses sat around tables immersed in conversation and laughter.

Danai recognised the queens and princesses and some other dignitaries. These were the elite of Bagumi, members of the noble houses who governed the kingdom, about fifty in all. Their children were the ones being entertained in the temporary fun park outside.

"Amara! You're here." Isha, the oldest Saene princess, sashayed through the aisle and wrapped Amara in a hug.

"Isha, it's so good to see you." Amara stepped into the other woman's embrace and kissed her cheek.

Danai moved back. No need to stay. She'd delivered the Nigerian princess to the party safely. So, she would wait outside with all the other bodyguards.

"Did you bring a guest?" Isha pulled back, looking in Danai's direction.

Danai glanced around, wondering who the princess was talking about. There was no one standing beside her.

"I didn't. That's your brother's new personal bodyguard." Amara didn't even swivel but continued walking deeper into the room, greeting the other attendees.

"Oh." Isha tilted her head, staring curiously. Then she stepped up to Danai. "You're Zawadi's new PPO?"

"Yes, First Princess. I'm Danai." She curtsied as butterflies fluttered in her belly.

The princess was one of Danai's heroes and a powerhouse of African womanism. They were the same age, and the woman had accomplished a lot.

Princess Isha was credited with being instrumental in ousting the thirty-five-year brutal regime of the former Wanaian dictator, Doona and ending the genocide of the Ganuri people. She also helped get her husband, Professor Zain Bassong elected as the new president of the Republic of Wanai.

Her intervention meant that all the guilty parties in the Ganuri genocide were arrested and undergoing court trials.

"It's nice to meet you, Danai," Isha beamed with a friendly smile. "So, where's my brother hiding this afternoon?"

Danai's breath hitched at the woman's familiarity, and she couldn't help the returning smile. It seemed the princess knew her brother too well. "He's in the library, enjoying the peace and quiet."

Isha's laughter tinkled. "Of course. Well, he'll be fine by himself. Join us for the party."

Isha placed her hands on Danai's shoulder, steering her towards the groups of women.

Danai resisted. "Princess, I'm not a party guest. I'm just here as a bodyguard."

"Nonsense. This event is open to every woman in the palace. We're celebrating the coming of the king's next grandchild. So, since you're here, you can join in. Yes?" Isha's brown eyes bore into her with expectations.

Danai should argue that she wasn't dressed for the occasion or remotely interested in hanging out with these women. She was more comfortable in a garage full of damaged cars and men in grease-stained overalls than she was in a banquet hall full of well-heeled ladies in sparkling jewellery.

Hell, she would rather spend the afternoon on a rugby field with sweaty, aggressive testosterone-laden men than be here.

But she had the utmost respect for Princess Isha, and if the woman thought it was right for Danai to be here, who was she to argue?

"Thank you, Your Highness." She allowed herself to be steered toward the dais where the elegantly dressed Queens Zulekha and Sapphire sat with the radiantly pregnant Princess Riona and the newly arrived Princess Amara.

Meanwhile, the king's daughters and Zareb's spouse sat at different tables away from the dais.

Princess India as the wife of the head of state of Sudar, sat with the Sudarese delegates while Princess Amira was with a group that included women Danai didn't recognise.

Danai knew about the attendees because she'd seen the guest list, and they'd been security cleared before the event. She could understand the pregnant princess staying on the dais with the king's consorts since it was her baby shower. But was the Nigerian princess such an esteemed guest to be seated with the queens? She supposed being engaged to the crown prince elevated Princess Amara's status in this gathering.

"You can sit at my table." Princess Isha pointed at a Wanaian delegates' table.

"Thank you." Danai recognised a familiar face. She'd met the woman months ago when they'd delivered a captured Kweku to the Wanaian security services. "Hello, Latifah."

# CHAPTER THIRTEEN

"Good morning, Ms Ruga," Zawadi said as he stepped outside his apartment and saw his PPO standing at attention.

"Good morning, Your Highness." She was dressed in the usual trousers and blazer combo, in navy-blue, with a white shirt and matching leather sneakers. "May I say. You sound ecstatic. Did something happen?"

"Nothing happened. I just had a very restful night. And it was wonderful to spend yesterday evening with all my siblings under one roof for the first time in a few years. Actually, it's the first time we've been together since Isha's wedding."

"That must have been wonderful."

"It was. I finally met Isha's adoptive children. Ifeh is a quiet, introspective eleven-year-old who reminds me of myself at that age, and Nadia is a precocious princess at six years old."

"Yes. I met them. They are lovely children."

"Oh. You met them." He grinned. "It seems you survived the day with children after all. You didn't break out in hives."

Her laughter tinkled and sent a sizzle down his spine. "I'll admit I'd never spent the day with so many women in one room. But I survived it, and no, I didn't break out in hives."

"That's good because I want to ask a favour."

"What is it?"

"My sister-in-law, Riona, asked if it was okay for you to be her protective escort when she visits the maternity suite."

Danai halted. "She requested me?"

"Yes. Is that a problem?"

"Not really…" she frowned.

"You will be doing me a favour."

She sighed. "Okay. Yes, I'll do it. When is the baby due?"

"Not for another month or so. But I will arrange for a room to be assigned to you in the palace so you will be close enough in case she has to make the trip in the middle of the night."

"Sure."

When they reached his office. Ms Ruga went in and did her usual checks. Before she stepped out, he said, "Thank you."

She smiled. "You're welcome."

Monday was back to business as usual. He'd just finished a briefing with the health minister about a SARS-type virus with a rapid infection rate and was spreading across Asia and Europe. The minister said they were seeking guidelines from the World Health Organisation and would keep him updated.

Now he sat in his office overlooking the courtyard garden. Nathan sat on the other side of the large desk.

"Have we covered everything?" Zawadi asked his assistant.

"There is one more thing, Your Highness." Nathan shifted in his seat. "There is an unsettling rumour floating around the palace that a female has joined The Royal Princes' rugby team."

Zawadi lifted his gaze from the document he'd been reading on his tablet, his spine stiffening in unexpected annoyance.

His assistant was his eyes and ears amongst the palace staff and brought him information about issues he needed to sort out.

So, his irritation at hearing the 'unsettling rumour' expression was odd. He usually dealt with stories with detachment. However, this one was about his PPO.

Danai—Ms Ruga, he corrected.

She currently stood just outside his office door. Just as she'd done every day since her arrival except on her days off work.

He remembered yesterday. The awareness that prickled his skin when she'd entered the palace library. He'd sensed her before she'd come into view, and warmth had flooded his body.

He'd refused to look up, refused to acknowledge his pulse rate accelerating until she'd presented and greeted him.

When he'd lifted his gaze and met hers, he'd been hit by the way her eyes had widened, glittering with feminine awareness. She'd been dressed in the navy blazer and pants suit, a white shirt underneath and navy-white leather sneakers on her feet. Yet her beautiful body had been evident.

He'd fought to maintain his legendary control. And had been relieved when Amara had arrived, surprising him. He'd been reminded of his obligations to his family and to his country.

His impending marriage to the Nigerian princess was not a love match, not the same way as his twin brothers' unions to their spouses.

Zawadi was the crown prince, the future king, and therefore couldn't afford the luxury of seeking frivolous romantic encounters. It was on his shoulders to secure the future of the Saene heritage by producing the next heir. So, his betrothal to Amara was about securing the future of Bagumi.

Still, he'd vowed to commit himself to the union just as his father devoted himself to the partnership with his mother.

But your father also made a love match with Queen Sapphire.

A faint ache made his temples throb. Zawadi squeezed his eyes shut, rubbing his clasped hands along the bridge of his nose. He wasn't his father.

"Your Highness?" Nathan's worried voice cut into his reverie.

Zawadi opened his eyes and dropped his hands palms-down on the table. "The rumours are true. Azikiwe recruited Ms Ruga to our rugby team."

His chest tightened with a twinge of guilt because he'd passed the buck to Zik. But he could've vetoed Zik's choice if he'd wanted. Honestly, Zawadi was excited to have Ms Ruga on their team. If their training sessions were anything to go by, she was in excellent form as a rugby player. It was a shame their country didn't have a national female squad because Ms Ruga would be in it.

"Oh." Nathan seemed lost for words.

Zawadi's irritation ramped up. "Why is the news unsettling?"

His assistant shifted uncomfortably, probably sensing his annoyance. "Your Highness, please forgive my impertinence. But males and females are segregated for sports. Also, Bagumi's morality and decency laws prohibit such activities."

The words exacerbated his headache. He really didn't need this extra problem with everything else going on.

"The Morality and Decency clauses apply to public events. So, of course, Ms Ruga will not play for our team in a public game. However, the Princes Vs Guards match is a closed-door event taking place on private property. The public is not invited."

"Okay. That makes sense. But what about the issue of Ms Ruga as a member of the fairer sex. Fielding her with eleven other men in the squad, not to mention the opposition team, would put her in danger of serious injury."

Zawadi's heart jolted. Nathan had a point.

The men in the squad were over one hundred kilograms each, while Danai was only sixty-nine kilos from her weigh-in last weekend. One lousy tackle, and she could be seriously injured.

The image of Danai in a crumpled broken heap on the rugby field flooded his mind.

His heart raced, his limbs weakening.

Maybe having her on the team was a bad idea. Should he boot her from the club? Yet, the idea didn't seem right.

Damn. He didn't want her getting hurt.

He swallowed the lump in his throat before speaking. "Thank you for bringing the issue to my attention. I will give it some consideration."

"Of course, Your Highness." Nathan straightened and bowed before walking out of the office.

As soon as the door closed, Zawadi pulled out his phone and sent a message to Zik.

Something came up. Do you have time this evening to discuss?

***

"What's got you so wound up?" Zik asked, climbing onto the tall, padded leather stool next to the bar.

Zawadi settled next to him on another stool. They were the only ones in the palace man cave tonight.

Zediah was less reluctant to be away from his pregnant wife. Zareb was always eager to go home to his new fiancée.

With Zawadi's formal betrothal to Amara, Zik was the only bachelor left in the royal family.

"We might have to remove Ms Ruga from the rugby squad," Zawadi said quietly.

"Why? I thought we resolved this. That woman is a pro player." Zik reared back.

"Have you considered how risky it is for her to play against men? I can't let her get injured."

A weird expression crossed Zik's face. "You can't let her get hurt? Hang on. You do realise she signed up to protect you. To take a bullet for you."

"I know. But it's not the same thing." Zawadi couldn't hide his agitation. "I've looked at the weight stats across the team, and we're at least thirty kilos heavier than her. You know the guards have men who weigh much more. Abdul is easily 140 kg. One bad tackle, and she could be hospitalised or worse. I can't let that happen."

"I see," Zik said, and silence fell upon them as they sipped the fruit-infused chilled water. "I think there's a way around this, and it involves the gameplay. Remember the tactic we used when Ekene was injured, and we had to keep the field clear for him."

"You mean we let her play and make her untouchable."

"Yes. You know she's a sprinter. Give her the ball, and she will fly."

"And the rest of us have to make sure the field is clear, and she doesn't get caught and tackled."

"Absolutely. PTQ."

"PTQ?"

"Protect The Queen. Danai is the queen in our game. The rest of us need to protect her and keep her in play because that's the only way we're going to win."

Zawadi grinned, some of his worries easing. The term was corny, but he liked it. This could work as long as they used the PTQ strategy. But he was nothing if not thorough. "Order a headguard for her anyway. Just in case she gets knocked over."

"Aye aye, captain." Zik saluted with a wink.

***

The rest of the week went in a flurry of activities. Zawadi thought he had a handle on the rugby squad situation.

On Saturday, he ran through the gameplay with everyone in the team, and they practised the PTQ strategy, which seemed to go smoothly.

However, when he returned to his apartment during the afternoon break, he had a summons to his mother's suite. He showered and changed into a long brown silk tunic and trouser set.

His parent understood his Saturdays were spent on the training grounds, so by requesting his presence, the matter had to be urgent.

At this time of the year, their parents were usually at the Lake Miri residence. But his mother had chosen to stay in DP because Zediah's second child was due any moment. Since she missed the birth of her first grandchild, she didn't want to miss this one.

When he arrived at her quarters, the uniformed guard who stood outside knocked and announced his presence.

He entered the spacious, lavishly designed antechamber and bowed. "Long live, Your Majesty."

Queen Zulekha, dressed in an elegant green gown, sat regally on a 17th Century Versailles style maroon and gold leaf upholstered settee framed in intricately carved mahogany wood. The intricate patterns and design blended with the sophisticated palatial ambience of the reception room—white flowers in gilded white vases sitting on Gold Leaf finished mahogany tables.

"Come, My Pride," his mother patted the sofa, indicating for him to join her.

He stepped forward, kissed the soft cheek she proffered before settling on the padded seat. These one-to-one moments with his mother were rare, but he cherished them. "Thank you, Mama. You wanted to see me?"

"Yes. You just completed your rugby training session?"

"Yes. Mother."

"What is this I hear that your female security operative is included in the team? Is that correct?"

"That is correct. Ms Ruga is a great addition to our team."

"Did Nathan speak to you?"

"About what?"

"About Ms Ruga and the rugby team."

"Yes, he spoke to me and raised some concerns. I said I would give them some consideration."

"And yet Ms Ruga was playing with you and the men today."

"Yes, she was. Mother, did you send Nathan to speak to me."

"Yes. I did. I was trying to be subtle."

"But subtlety is not your style."

"Obviously. It didn't work, which is why I summoned you this afternoon."

"Mother, you've never taken an interest in rugby sports or my involvement with it. Why the interest now?"

His mother reached across and covered his hand with hers. Zawadi was not tactile. Neither was his mother, one of the things they had in common. So, the physical contact, whilst not unwelcome, was strange.

Something was troubling his mother.

"What is it?"

"Do you know why I call you My Pride?"

"No, Mama." His mother only used the expression when they were in private like this. He'd never questioned it and just assumed it was her way of showing her love for him.

"You know this already. But early in my marriage contract with your father, I knew the king was in love with Sapphire. He wanted to marry her. Although we were attracted to each other, our match was a political one. I know your father felt he had little choice but to wed me at the time to avoid making enemies of my people.

To be fair, I wanted to marry your father. I had been raised to be a queen, and he was a king. We had a nation to govern together. So, when he revealed his love for another woman, I knew that marrying her would be inevitable. Still, I was hurt."

"I'm sorry, Mama. If you were unhappy, why didn't you divorce him?"

His mother huffed an unamused smile. "Why should I? I am a queen. Why should I give it up to someone else? Divorce was not an option I would've considered. Ibrahim's father had married multiple wives. Therefore, I expected your father might do the same. So, I set some conditions. Your father was not permitted to marry again until I had borne the heir. Almighty heard my prayers, and within a few weeks of being married, you were conceived. And when you arrived and proved to be a male child, my heart swelled with pride, which is why I call you My

Pride. Your arrival validated and vindicated my actions."

He squeezed his mother's hand. "Why are you telling me this now?"

"Because your dalliance with Ms Ruga concerns me."

"Mother, it is not a dalliance. She is an employee, and I would never—"

She raised her hand. "Hear me out. There is a saying about 'what an elder sees while sitting, a child cannot see while at the top of the tallest tree'. I see history repeating itself, and I want to stop it from happening."

Zawadi puffed out a sigh. His mother was bent on speaking her mind, and he just had to let her.

"You and Ms Ruga. I saw both of you the other morning as she walked you from your apartment to the office. I was having morning tea with the balcony doors open. Your laughter and conversation drew my attention. The softness of your voice, the way you looked at each other. I'd seen that expression before. It's exactly how your father is with Sapphire."

"What does that even mean?"

"It means something is going on between you and Ms Ruga."

"There's nothing."

"Remember what I said about seeing things you can't. Look, your wedding to Amara is six months away. We don't want anything to jeopardise it. So, here's what we'll do. I have Amara's confidence. I will speak to her and prepare her for the possibility of you marrying a second wife in the near future."

"What?" Zawadi's throat locked in horror.

His mother raised her hand in censure. "But I will offer her the same deal I made your father. She will bear the heir before you can marry another wife—"

"Mother, I'm going to stop you right there." This train had gone off the tracks. "You will do no such thing. I'm going to marry Amara, and with time hopefully, love will grow between us. Aside from that, I have no intentions of marrying anyone else. If you're so concerned about Ms Ruga being in the team. After the upcoming game, I will sack her from the team." His stomach rolled at the words, but he had to say them. "And I promise to limit my interaction with Ms Ruga to just work-related so no one will misconstrue my actions towards her. I'm not in love with Ms Ruga. I don't even know what that is."

His mother puffed out a breath and nodded. "Very well. Let it be so."

# CHAPTER FOURTEEN

*March 2020*

The Princes Vs Guards Match Day came around quick enough. Although it was a private event held in the palace sports field with only staff, members of the royal family and their friends watching, excitement still buzzed in the air.

Ahead of the required time, Danai left her suite, her sports bag over her shoulder and walked towards the gymnasium. Through the palace were new faces she didn't recognise.

Because twelve guards would be on the playing field and many other palace employees would be there to watch the game, the Royal Reserves were here to secure the place for the day. They were everywhere.

The gymnasium was filled with activities.

"There you are," Zik said as she approached. "How do you feel?"

"I'm quite hyped. Is everyone here?"

He grinned. "Great. Pretty much. Ekene and Ejike should be here soon."

"Those are Princess Amara's brothers, right?"

"Yes. But they're also my good friends. That would be them now." The sound of a helicopter filled the air. "Head to the changing room. I'll join you shortly."

"Okay." Danai walked through the doors into the corridor. More Royal Reserves stood outside the entrances. She halted when she saw the sign over the female shower rooms now read 'Royal Guards'.

They had a problem. If the guards were in her standard changing room, where was she supposed to change? The sign over the male bathrooms read 'Royal Princes'.

Since she was an honorary prince regarding the rugby team, she would have to change with them. But she couldn't just walk in without warning them of her presence. So, she knocked on the door.

A few seconds later, it was pulled back, and Razi stood in front of her. "Oh, it's you, Danai. Come in."

Flabbergasted, she muttered, "Eh, don't you want to warn the others..." so they can cover up, she didn't add.

"Why? You're part of the team." He moved out of the way, and she stepped into the changing room.

Ten men were in various stages of dressing. They shouted out greetings as she walked in and carried on with what they were doing.

Prince Zareb was fully clothed, talking to the team coach, who wore the team sweats and jacket.

Prince Zawadi sat on a bench, already in the shorts and jersey, pulling on his socks. He glanced at her, but his expression was blank.

"You're in there." Razi pointed at a cubicle, drawing her attention.

She hurried to it and paused to read the piece of paper stuck on it. Her name was typed out in bold capital letters. But someone had scribbled 'The Queen' in black pen under her name, so it read:

DANAI

(The Queen)

Cheeks flaming, she glanced around the space, but no one was looking at her. Who would have done such a thing? It was probably a joke, and the culprit could be Razi or Zik. They were the two jokesters in the team.

She stepped into the cubicle, shut the door, and flipped the metal bolt.

"Warm-up is in fifteen minutes," the coach's voice boomed louder than the other voices.

Danai focused her attention on getting changed.

The sounds outside the cubicle got louder. Zik had entered with the two Nigerian princes.

Once changed. Danai took her bag and left the enclosure. The men were dressed in team gears and moved into a huddle as the coach outlined the starting seven and the substitutes.

Danai was a substitute. She didn't mind. It would give her time to watch the rival team and see how they played to prepare herself.

The coach gave his pep talk, they pulled into a huddle, and one of them said a quick prayer before they dispersed, heading out.

"Here," Zawadi said and opened one of the wooden lockers. "You can put your bag in here."

He took a protective black headguard out. "Zik ordered this for you. We didn't want you suffering a head injury."

"Oh. Thank you." She took it and strapped it on. There was a space to pull her braids into a ponytail. "It's really considerate of you."

"No. Thank you for doing this. We appreciate it, and we're going to protect you."

Emotion made her throat clog up, and warmth spread through her body. She forgot everything else as their gazes connected and locked.

Standing this close to him, it was impossible to miss the compelling back eyes, the firm features of his face and the confident set of his broad shoulders. Nor could she ignore the way the jersey stretched across his toned chest and revealed the muscular arms.

His body oozed power, strength. It seemed to be such a contrast from the prince she'd seen by an alcove in the library weeks ago. Now she was staring at Zawadi, the jock. Regardless of whether he was a scholar or an athlete, he was super sexy.

She became aware of the strength of her heartbeats, and her mouth watered. She must have stepped close because they were only inches apart and his scent filled her nostrils.

The squeaking door broke the spell, and she stepped back.

"Are you guys coming?" Razi called out from the doorway.

"We are." Zawadi strode towards the exit and held it open for her. "Are you ready?"

"I am. Let's do this." She stepped into the corridor. Sunlight streaked in through the double doors.

As she jogged to the pitch, a big cheer erupted. Danai almost stumbled in shock but righted herself before she could faceplant on the turf.

People lined the edges of the grounds. It seemed every palace employee was here as a spectator. The players were also allowed to invite their spouses or significant others. She'd sent the private invitation to Oumou and Yahya. She'd received a text message when they'd arrived and had been ushered through the security. Stacked sitting areas had been erected over the past week to expand on the already existing sheltered dugouts. There were security personnel patrolling the grounds.

Danai realised the cheers were not for her. Prince Zawadi was behind her, and they were cheering for him.

She ran up to the rest of the team, who occupied one half of the pitch while the guards were in the other half. The referee and the other officials spoke to each group for a few minutes.

They spent the next thirty minutes following the pre-match warm-up routine established during their training sessions. It helped to prepare them mentally as well as physically for the game.

Then Danai and the other substitutes, the coach, and the physiotherapy team returned to the benches in the dugout. Prince Zawadi made a short speech, the referee blew the whistle, and the match began.

Rugby Sevens was a variant of the rugby union game, fielding seven players for seven-minute halves. However, the pace of the game was faster with quicker scrums and fewer restarts.

The first team was Zawadi, Zik, Zareb, Ejike, Ekene, Razi, and Osei, an Asante royal prince. Danai and four other men, friends of the princes, made up the squad of twelve.

The opposition initial line-up was Abdul, Amadu, Yusuf, Pierre, Harry, a guard whose name she'd forgotten and Kojo, who was Princess Isha's bodyguard. He no longer lived in the palace but had arrived from Wanai last night.

Both sides made tries quite early. The spectators cheered with each score regardless of the team. Midway through the first half, the princes were ahead because they had converted all their tries, but the guards had missed one kick.

"You're up," the coach said to Danai.

She straightened and started warming up along the touchline. About a minute later, Ekene jogged across the touchline and tagged Danai as his substitute. Then, she raced onto the pitch.

Zawadi looked at her and indicated where she should go, and she got into the wing position as the ball was still in play. Zareb retrieved the ball from the scrum and passed it on to Zik, who tossed it at Danai, and she exploded into a run for the opposing goal line. When she had men who were almost twice her weight chasing her down, she had no other option but to power through the sprint. She narrowly avoided a tackle and crashed across the line with a try.

The stadium exploded with cheers as her team hugged her in celebration.

Danai was ecstatic. She'd scored on her first touch. Probably because she was still full of energy, and the men were burning out.

Zik converted the try with a drop goal, increasing their lead by seven points. Then, he kicked off for the restart, and Danai was in the flow of the game.

At half-time, they had two minutes break, which gave her time to grab a drink. Then they were back in a huddle and getting a pep talk from Coach.

The second half started, and she was substituted by Ekene. A fumble by Osei meant that Royal Guards equalised with a try and a conversion. The scores stayed level for the next few minutes until Ekene tagged Danai again.

As soon as Danai got the ball and started running, someone tackled her, knocking the breath out of her, and she tumbled over, blanking out for a moment.

When she opened her eyes, the team surrounded her.

Zawadi stooped next to her, his gaze pained, his brows furrowed in a worried expression. He was on her right side, left hand up. "Danai, how many fingers am I holding up?"

She blinked to clear her vision. "Three fingers."

"You blanked out for a few seconds. How are you feeling?" The physio's voice made her turn.

"I'm feeling fine. If you can just help me up," she replied.

He reached out and pulled her up. The crowd cheered.

The referee checked her before giving a yellow card to Yusuf, who had made a bad tackle and sent him to the sin bin for two minutes.

Zik kicked the penalty earning Royal Princes three points and taking them ahead. Then he kicked off the restart. With the guards one man down, the princes scored a try and a conversion taking them ten points ahead when the full-time whistle sounded.

Time flew in a haze of congratulations and cheers. Prince Zawadi gave another speech thanking the guards for outstanding sportsmanship and the spectators for showing up. He invited everyone to the party in the gym lounge afterwards. Everyone had earned an afternoon off work.

Danai spent time chatting with some of the female palace employees who approached her. They found it fascinating that a woman had played rugby with an all-male team. They asked if Danai thought this would catch on, and the sports would become a unisex team.

Danai doubted it and explained why the physiological differences between the genders would make that impossible for some sports.

By the time she returned to the changing room, guards were standing outside. Most of the men had showered and were dressing. The post-match buzz and energy were still high. Zik and the other princes were talking about a place they would head to this evening.

"You're coming with us to the afterparty, Danai," Ekene said, who was towelling his wet, naked body.

"I am?" Danai tried to avert her gaze, but there were practically naked bodies everywhere she turned. Still, she was flabbergasted that they would invite her to their festivities. These people were royalty, and she was not in their league.

"Yes, I'm taking every member of the team out, and you are a member of this team," Zik said. He had a towel slung around his hips.

These men had no body shame. Then again, they were all good looking, fit young men with wealth and status.

What was there to be ashamed of?

She hadn't seen the crown prince since she entered the changing rooms. He might still be in the shower.

"Is Zawadi coming too?" she asked. She was allowed to address them informally within the sports field and the gym.

"My brothers are not party animals. They tend to be damp squids. Say you'll join us. Pretty please." Zik gave her a puppy-eyed look.

She chuckled, understanding why people never said no to him. "Sure."

"Yay!" He cheered as the other men laughed.

Danai went to the locker, grabbed toiletries and a towel before heading to the showers. Thankfully they were partitioned into a row of eight units with lockable opaque glass doors providing privacy.

One of the cubicles was closed and the shower running. Probably Prince Zawadi.

She imagined his naked body with rivulets of water cascading over him. Heart jolting with awareness, she walked into the first, shut it and started undressing.

The urge to talk to him from across the cubicles sizzled down her spine. She wanted to thank him for letting her play the game, for including her in the team.

The water shut off from the other unit. There was rustling, and about a minute later, the person left the cubicle. Footsteps faded as the person departed.

Hair covered with a shower cap, she turned on the faucet, and water rained down. She grabbed her gel, scrubbed her body with the loofah and rinsed it off. Then she closed the tap, dried her body, and wrapped the towel over her breasts before exiting the showers.

The locker room was quiet, almost empty.

Prince Zawadi pulled his vest over his head. His abdominal muscles rippled. His trousers slung low on his hips, and a dark trail of short curly hair disappeared into the edge of his cotton boxers.

He tucked his vest into his trousers and looked up. "Danai?"

Her cheeks flamed. He'd caught her ogling. "Sorry. I didn't realise you would be here."

She hurried towards the cubicle with her name on it, stopping to grab her bag from the locker. She shut the door and proceeded to dress quickly, determined not to think about the prince or the continued obsession she had for him.

He would never see her as anything more than his PPO.

She would find Oumou and Yahya and get something to eat. She missed her family and hadn't seen them for the past month.

Dressed in jeans, a t-shirt, and sneakers, she stepped out of the cubicle and halted.

The crown prince sat on a bench, elbows on thighs, chin on the tips of his clasped hands. He straightened as she exited. "Ms Ruga, I'd like to talk to you."

The formal way he said her name sent a cold shiver down her spine. Something was wrong.

"Yes, Your Highness." She responded equally in a formal tone, although this was a space where formality was banned.

"Please, sit." He pointed at the opposite bench.

She lowered her body onto it, keeping her bag next to her. "Is everything alright?"

He met her gaze, but she couldn't read his expression. "First of all, I want to congratulate and thank you for a job well done. You played excellently today. It's easy to see that you are one of the best players we've had in the team."

"I appreciate your kind words. Thank you."

He nodded. "With that in mind. Please don't think this has anything to do with your ability to play rugby because it doesn't. However, unfortunately, I have to dismiss you from the team."

"Oh." At first, shock ran through her. Then the embers of anger flared. "Why?"

"I can't say."

"You can't say?" She jerked upright. "You sack me from the team, and you won't tell me why? To hell with this."

She grabbed her bag and stormed out.

# CHAPTER FIFTEEN

About five minutes after Danai stormed out of the changing rooms, Zawadi carried his leather sports kit towards the door only to have it nearly slammed in his face.

He jerked out of the way in time as Azikiwe barrelled in, his expression thunderous. "What the hell have you done?"

Zawadi averted his gaze. Guilt thickened his throat, and his voice cracked. "Is this about Ms Ruga?"

"Yes." His brother braced his hands on his hips, legs wide apart. "What did you do to her?"

Zawadi lowered his butt to the nearest bench and stared at his feet, head bowed. His stomach felt loose and unsettled.

"I sacked her from the team," he said, his voice heavy, this tone sombre.

"Why the hell would you do such a thing? She was one of the best players on that pitch today. She was the 'man of the match', and you know it. We haven't beaten the guards by such a margin for a very long time."

"I know. She was brilliant." He lifted his head, staring at the far wall. His adrenaline spiked as he remembered Danai's gameplay. "Every time she touched the ball, she was like a rocket powering towards that goal line. She was compelling to watch."

He couldn't help the awe in his voice as his body temperature rose and his skin tingled.

"Exactly. So why would you kick her off the team? And today of all days. You couldn't even let her enjoy the win." The accusation in his brother's voice matched his indicting expression.

Zawadi didn't need his brother denunciation to know that he had messed up. He felt shitty already. "You're right. I should have waited a few days before telling her she was off the team. I was wrong to announce it today."

Zik huffed out a breath. "It still doesn't explain why she is off the team."

Zawadi rubbed his knuckles along the bridge of his nose as a headache bloomed. "Did you not see that she was nearly injured today? Next time could be worse."

Azikiwe settled on the opposite bench, his posture less combative. "But we have a strategy to keep her safe, and it works. Anyway, I saw you talking to Yusuf after the game. I'm sure you told him to back off on her."

The dread from seeing Danai tackled to the ground returned. When she'd blanked out for a few seconds on the pitch, he'd been worried she had been knocked unconscious. He'd never worried about any of his teammates in the same manner. So, his relief when she'd stood and walked by herself had been palpable. Still, he'd had to scold the guards' team captain for the dangerous attack on Danai.

"Yes. I told Yusuf to ensure that his team keeps it clean for future matches. But don't you see that it is wrong for me to do it. How many other teams am I going to warn about restraining from bad tackles? We have the Rugby Sevens festival coming in a few months. We play about six matches on the day with six different teams. Should I warn each of those teams to go easy on her?"

"No. You don't have to warn any teams. They will all meet us head-on as usual. I'm sure she appreciates that you're concerned about her wellbeing. But Danai is not weak. She's mentally and physically powerful. For goodness sakes, the woman signed up to take a bullet for you. Give her some credit." Zik's posture matched Zawadi, and he lowered his voice. "But something tells me there's more to the reason why you want her out of harm's way."

Zawadi stiffened, feeling attacked. "What other reason do I need?"

"Maybe because you care about her."

"Of course, I care about her. The same way I care about other employees," He muttered as heat rose from his chest to his face. His mother had accused him of the same thing.

"Not just as an employee. She means more to you. Like a lover."

"No." Zawadi shot off the bench. "Of course not. I'm already engaged. I'm not like you."

"What do you mean you're not like me? What's wrong with me?"

"Nothing. I mean, you're good with women. You know how to handle them. Considering the number of women you've been associated with, I thought we would've received complaints about you. Instead, according to the palace PR team, your social media accounts get hundreds of new followers every day."

"Perhaps you should be more like me. First, I would never lie to a woman about the way they make me feel. If you say A and you mean B, it's going to backfire."

"But I haven't told any lies."

"When you refuse to confront the way you feel about Danai, you're lying to yourself and to her inadvertently."

"But..." he trailed off, unable to string words together and produce a rebuttal.

"Let me ask you one thing, and it's just between the two of us."

"Yes?"

"Are you attracted to her?"

"Well, yes. She's a beautiful woman."

"Do you find yourself thinking about her when she's not there? Be honest."

Damn. His brother was bent on making him confront repressed emotions.

"Yes," he barked grumpily.

"If you wake up tomorrow and she wasn't here. And you found out she was gone and would not return. Would you miss her presence?"

His chest squeezed tight. He looked forward to every morning when he would step outside his apartment door and find Ms Ruga standing there waiting for him. A thrill usually crept up his spine, and warmth spread across his chest. Their conversations as they walked to his office building. The smile on her face. The way her brown eyes sparkled about a topic she enjoyed.

"Yes, I would miss her presence," he answered honestly. "She has become a part of my daily routine."

"So, I will ask you this and be honest too. Are you kicking her off the team because you have feelings for her?"

Zawadi stiffened. Zik's words hit a little too close for comfort.

Seeing Danai in the changing room wrapped in only a towel after her shower had brought all his cravings for her to the fore. It had taken every ounce of willpower to not demolish the distance between them, tug the towel off her body and satisfy the desire burning in his veins.

When she'd grabbed her bag and locked herself in the cubicle, the spell had been broken. He'd sworn he wouldn't place himself in such a compromising position again, which meant she had to leave the squad.

"I'm kicking her off the team," he said stiffly. "Because having a woman on our team breaches our Morality and Decency Laws and could cause a scandal. Mama brought it to my attention, and she is right. We can't bring the Saene name to disrepute."

"I knew it," Zik exclaimed as if he had the answer to a complex conundrum. "I knew the high queen must have gotten to you. Do you know what?" Zik stood. "Once upon a time, I thought I was the People Pleaser around here. But it turns out, it's you."

Zawadi raised his hands in frustration. "What would you have me do? I'm engaged."

"Our father married two wives. I'm sure you'll figure it out." Zik walked of the door, slamming it in his wake.

Zawadi's mouth dropped open. Was Zik really telling him that he could wed two women just like their father had done? His mother had mentioned it too. Was that really an option for him?

# CHAPTER SIXTEEN

The Castle was a shock to Danai and yet, precisely apt.

They drove through a thunderstorm and rain for an hour from Darusa in a convoy of vehicles—sleek, sporty ones and blacked-out SUVs.

Danai sat in the back of one of the SUVs—the fourth in the column—with Oumou and Yahya as their headlights cut into the country lane bordered by grass. Then they drove through a copse of trees and a dark tunnel. On the other side was a long, gravelled driveway. A massive three-level mansion stood at the end of it.

Located at the foothills of the Beya Mountains, the mansion was built in the quadrangular style of ancient Bagumian homes crossed with a Medieval castle. It had been built as one of the gatehouses to the fortress castle carved into the mountain. It had sheltered the citizens from colonial invasion and the subsequent transatlantic slave trade.

There were rows of cars already parked outside, and security men ushered them inside.

A big sign read, "What happens in The Castle stays in The Castle." Under it, a male usher took their mobile phones and digital devices and stored them in small drawers in a vault and tagged armbands onto their wrists. No recordings or photographs were allowed.

Music thumped as welcome. The place had recently been modernised. The ceiling rose far above their heads as they walked into what would have been the banquet hall which now looked like a dark club with colourful lighting and a huge bar along the sidewall.

"Wow," Yahya said.

"This place is amazing." Oumou gasped.

"I need a drink," Danai said and walked to the bar and ordered double shots for them. She needed to shake off the anger eating away at her and didn't want to think about what had happened earlier after the rugby match. Soon the alcohol did its job, hazing her mind.

"Let's dance." She dragged Oumou to the packed dance floor, leaving Yahya by the bar.

"Thank you for bringing me here today. I needed this," her friend leaned close to speak in her ear.

"Me too." The music made her body sway, twirling with melody. It rushed through her skin, the drumbeats pounding in her chest, making her feel utterly free. Sexy. Powerful.

Oumou tipped her head back, eyes glazed as she danced. This was one thing they enjoyed doing whenever they could which was rare these days.

She should be worried about this den of debauchery. Concerned about the safety of the princes—between Zik and his regal friends, many African royal families would suffer significantly if something went wrong here.

But tonight, Danai was tired of being reasonable and controlled. She wanted to shed those things and lash out at all the restrictions on her life.

The frustrations of her job.

She could worry about repercussions tomorrow.

The alcohol rubbed away most of her anger, her annoyance fizzing away. Now, she felt warm and fuzzy, almost happy. A lazy smile made her cheeks ache, and her body moved with ease. Sweat dripped down her back, making the two-tone body-hugging leather dress stick to her body. It had cost her a few quid when she'd bought it, but it was one of the sexiest pieces of clothing she owned. It showed off her legs leading to her feet in the matching ankle boots. The air was thick and humid, although she could feel blasts of cold air from air-conditioners.

A group sat in a dark corner, smoking. The smell of marijuana mixed with the smell of alcohol and sweat. Technically she was law enforcement and should be confiscating drugs.

She didn't care. If Prince Zik didn't mind, why should she. Plus, she was under the influence of alcohol and was in no condition to arrest anyone.

Someone bumped into her, and she turned her head.

"Hey, Danai," Prince Osei said with a grin, his eyes glazed over. "Are you having fun?"

"Sure. And you?" she asked. He looked like he was having a great time.

"Absolutely." His gaze settled on Oumou. "Is this gorgeous human your sister? May I be introduced."

Oumou giggled, suddenly looking like a teenager instead of the boss lady that she was.

Danai shook her head as she smiled. "This is my step-sister, Oumou. This is Prince Osei."

"I'm just Osei tonight." He extended his arm. "It's my pleasure to meet you, Oumou."

"Mine too." Oumou placed her palm over his arm.

"I'm going to get a drink. Do you want any?" Danai asked.

Her friend just waved her off in response.

Danai grinned. At least her friend looked like she would have a happy ending tonight with a prince, which didn't seem to be on the cards for Danai. She headed to the bar but was intercepted by a stricken Yahya.

"What the fuck, cuz. Did you just introduce Oumou to that guy?"

"Yes. He wanted to meet her, and she seemed quite keen to meet him."

"Fuck." He scrubbed a hand over his face and stomped to the bar.

She followed, shaking her head. She climbed onto an available stool and reordered while he joined her.

"Cuz, what is really going on between you and Oumou."

"Nothing." He looked away.

"There's something. There has always been something. If you like her as much as I think you do. Why not ask her out like any normal human being?"

"Because nothing can come of it. You know her family background. My father found out I liked her and forbade me from getting involved with her."

Anger made Danai's blood boil. Her uncle Hissene was a tyrant. He was domineering and liked to control everything.

"Why the hell are you still listening to your father? You can't believe all that nonsense superstition. My father married Oumou's mother, and they are happy together. What's going to stop you from being happy with her?"

"I don't know, cuz. It's not as simple as you make it."

"Because you're making it complicated. Just go up to her and confess your feelings. I'm sure she would rather be with you than with a prince."

Yahya grimaced. "Are you serious? I'm a mechanic. He's the son of a Ghanaian king. No contest."

"Men. You are so stupid sometimes." She got off the stool with her drink. But froze when her neck prickled.

Darkness swamped the lounge interspersed with intermitted colourful lighting. Silhouettes moved, swaying, kissing, dancing, even sexing. It seemed some people had no shame about public displays in here, and anything went.

Still, through it all, one body stood out, like a rainbow through grey clouds, making everyone else fade into obscurity. The dark-rimmed spectacles seemed to amplify the onyx eyes that were laser fixed on her. He was in a shiny, black tunic-and-trousers set with gold embroidery around the collar and cuffs. Even in this place saturated with nobility and the highborn, there was no mistaking his regality. He stood above the rest.

Her breath hitched. A wicked smile tugged her lips, and her stomach fluttered into her chest.

Prince Zawadi was here. He'd come here. She hadn't thought he would be here. This kind of depravity didn't seem like his cup of tea.

Prince Zik was saying something to him and gesticulating, but Zawadi didn't look away from her. Instead, Zik glanced in her direction, shrugged, and walked away.

The music changed to a slower sultry rhythm. Her nerves tingled as a guy came up behind her, bumping and rubbing sensually against her.

Somewhere inside her, a warning flashed to move away from the stranger. Yet, she didn't. Instead, she swayed her hips, lifted the hair off her neck as the man wrapped an arm around her midriff, pulling her closer.

Even from across the room, she could feel Zawadi anger ripple across the space. She didn't care. He could go to Hell after what he did today.

She tipped her head back as the man nuzzled her neck. She wasn't even sure who he was as he hadn't spoken, and she hadn't glanced back.

It didn't matter who he was. He was here to serve one purpose.

To show the uptight Prince Zawadi that he couldn't control her. To show that she couldn't be beaten down by his ridiculous attitude. She would get laid and forget all about him.

Yet, somehow, her body couldn't forget about him. When she tilted her head to look in his direction, her heart slammed into her chest. He was only a few feet away and coming closer.

She straightened and said to the guy behind her, "Give me a minute."

The man reluctantly released her.

Zawadi stopped in front of her. Close enough to touch.

"Your Highness," she said.

"Danai," his voice was low, deep, and vibrating with anger.

It was as if he'd licked her skin. Her breath hitched, and her body shuddered. Damn. She needed him.

Without much thought, she took a step towards him.

"Is there something I can do for you?" There was no missing the suggestion in her sultry tone.

"There's something…" his words were slow and hoarse and full of challenge.

Her chest rose and fell as her breathing quickened. What was really going on? Was he going to say what she wanted to hear?

"You shouldn't be here." The timbre of his voice caused vibrations in her core.

"But you are here." Her throat tightened. Perhaps it was the alcohol. Maybe she didn't care anymore. Reason flew from her brain. Her feet carried her towards him.

"I'm here because of you." The way his stare bore into her as if she was everything. His very reason for existing. No one had ever looked at her like that before.

One chance. That's all she wanted. Was that so impossible?

"I was invited. We're celebrating a win. Remember?" she taunted him, stepping into his personal space.

Stiffening, he grimaced, and for the first time since she saw him, he broke eye contact, looking remorseful. "I'm sorry about earlier."

"That's all well and good. But am I back in the squad?" She tilted her chin up, getting in his face.

He sighed. "No."

"Then all is not forgiven." She moved closer until the soft fabric of his clothes brushed her bare legs. She kept her tone raspy and throaty. "So now that you're here, what do you want to do?"

Her fingers itched to touch him. To know how his skin felt. Her toes curled in her boots as they rubbed next to his black shoes. Suddenly she itched to feel him in a thousand ways.

She ghosted her hand over his tunic, barely grazing his chest and arms.

To hell with restraint. She placed her palms on his chest and glided it down, felt the heat of his skin soak into hers, felt the steady quickening rhythm of his pounding heartbeats through the silky fabric. His stomach muscles clenched as she trailed down his torso.

Her core tightened, her pulse racing. Touching him only inspired more craving within her body. Within her soul.

"Danai."

The husky way he said her name made her eyes flutter shut for a few seconds. It seemed to feed her craving with more fuel. Her breathing came faster. Her core throbbed for contact, slicking her thighs.

"What are you doing?" His question held censure. Yet, he didn't touch her or push her away. It was almost as if he was afraid of touching her. Afraid he would lose control.

She would help him along.

"You have to learn to relax. You're so stiff." She leaned in and spoke close to his ears. With her boots, they were the same height.

A groan rumbled through him.

"Why did you have to say stiff?" he muttered low, but she still heard it.

His erection pulsed through his trousers against her hip. "Oh."

Here was the proof that he was attracted to her even if he would never admit it. She rolled her hip, rubbing against him, shivers rippling through her.

"Danai," the warning was back in his voice but still didn't do anything physical to prevent her actions.

Obsession for him rippled through her. He hadn't told her to stop or tried to push her away. She would stop if he told her to do so.

In the meantime, she let the thumping music sway her. She danced against his body, winding her waist, dragging up and down his body, rolling her hips against his groin.

It was almost like dancing against a tree as he did nothing but stand there, hands clenched by his sides. His jaw was stern, his nose flaring. Damn, he smelled good.

Every contact with him burned her, desire searing a path to her core. His heavy erection pressing against her only made her core pulse with persistent need. Yearning for him to thrust into her again and again. A moan bubbled inside her, desperation clawing her skin. Maybe she could chase the orgasm right here. Nothing else seemed to matter in this space. The rest of the world was forgotten. They could live in this bubble, if only for a short while.

"Whatever happens in The Castle stays in The Castle. Give me one night," she said into his ear.

His entire body froze. "Danai, are you drunk?"

His question was a splash of cold water on the party mood and returned her flare of annoyance. "What the heck is the matter with you? Can you not have fun for once? Look around you. Everyone here is drunk or high or both."

She dropped her arms and turned away. Having Zawadi in her life any other way would never happen. All she'd wanted was one blissful night with him, and she couldn't even get that. What was the point in trying?

"Look at me," he ordered.

She ignored him and stepped back.

"Please, Danai." He sounded desperate. He brushed her arm, quick, brief, light. But still a blissful touch.

Something fluttered in her chest, and warmth spread through her. She turned back to him, a smile on her face as she wrapped her arms around him. "I know you're worried about me. But be certain that what I'm doing now is what I've always wanted to do. I'm sober enough to know that I want you. Have always wanted you."

He nodded, his expression softening as he tilted to examine her face. The way he stared at her made her stomach flip-flop like a rollercoaster.

"You will ruin me," he said in a low voice, his breath feathering her mouth where his gaze was focused.

Her emotions unravelled because she understood what he meant. He had so much to lose. But she didn't want him to give any of it up because of her.

She lifted her arms, threading fingers behind his neck, loving the feel of his skin and short hairs on his nape. "That's why I'm asking for just tonight. Nothing more."

"But you don't know what you're asking—"

She didn't let him finish. Allowed the craving to drive her actions, she leaned forward and grazed her lips against his.

"Stop."

The command jarred Danai out of the haze of lust, making her halt.

"Shit," Zawadi muttered under his breath as he bolted apart as if they'd been doing something inappropriate. His shoulders rose and arms clasped in front of him in his usual regal pose. He lifted his gaze, meeting hers, his expression stern and his mouth twisted in disapproval. "I cannot give you what you're asking. There can never be anything between us. Good night, Ms Ruga."

He swivelled and walked away.

Her stomach dropped, and it felt like her world collapsed as she watched his retreating back. Her throat clogged up.

Slowly she turned and walked back to the bar. She wasn't going to wallow in self-pity. She didn't care anyway, did she? She was only here on a mission. She would focus her attention on finding the palace mole. Once that was done, she would be gone. Back to her old life. Away from royalty.

And yet, her heart ached.

## CHAPTER SEVENTEEN

After Zawadi's departure, Danai, Oumou and Yahya retired for the night. She didn't feel like partying with the disappointment weighing her shoulders. It would have been better if Prince Zawadi had never come to The Castle. It was bad enough that he had ruined her post-match vibe. He'd also ruined the night for her.

A suite was assigned to them in The Castle. She and Oumou shared a bed while Yahya was on the sofa. Sleep came because of the alcohol in her body, but it was unsettled, and she was haunted by dreams of the crown prince.

Her cousin and stepsister returned to Bali first thing this morning, and Danai got back to Darusa Palace in time to shower and change before her phone pinged.

It was a message from Riona: Please come over to our apartment.

Maybe Prince Zediah's wife would be delivering the baby soon. She was nine months pregnant, and Danai had agreed to be her security for the delivery suite. Hence the text message.

Danai creamed her body and dressed quickly in her work clothes, although it was her day off. Since Riona messaged her, it had to be about work.

The palace seemed eerily quiet even at this time of the morning, considering yesterday's sporting event and celebrations.

At Zediah's apartment, the guard outside knocked and let her in. She walked into the foyer of the four-bed apartment.

Zediah came out of the living room. "Oh, you're here. Riona had a restless night. I think she should go to the hospital. I've called the maternity unit, and they say they are prepared for her."

He ushered her into the living room, where Riona sat on one of the sofas.

Danai had been in the apartment before. The household had seemed chaotic, with Nour running around the place shadowed by the nanny. Toys everywhere. Prince Zediah fussing over his wife nonstop.

Now it seemed calmer and tidier, although the prince was still a fusspot.

"Hi, Princess. Is everything okay?" Danai asked. She liked the woman who had been quite lovely during the baby shower event.

"Yes. I'm sorry you had to wake up so early. I told Zed we had plenty of time. But he's restless, and it's wearing me out." She nodded in her husband's direction.

The man was pacing the living room and at risk of wearing a path into the rug.

Danai hid her smile. The man was like a mother hen. She turned her attention to the calm Riona. "Would you like to head to the hospital?"

"Now, you're here. Yes. I didn't want to go without you."

Danai was honoured that the woman thought she was important. She wasn't a midwife and had never witnessed a live birth. Yet somehow, the woman trusted her presence and judgement. Trusted her protection skills.

"Okay. We'll get you there safely. Is your bag packed?"

"Over there." The princess indicated a large leather overnight bag in the corner.

"Good. Prince Zediah, have you informed the chauffeur?" Danai couldn't allow the already wound-up prince to drive. She couldn't operate the vehicle herself since she was security and would have to enter the hospital with the princess.

"Yes. He is on standby," the man replied.

"Okay. Let him know we're on the way down and grab the bag. Let me help you up, Princess."

The woman smiled as Danai took her hand and helped her while she pushed off the sofa. She took the smile to mean that Danai was doing the right things by controlling the situation.

There was light rain and fog with an overcast sky as they left the palace. The hospital was only fifteen minutes away.

The private suite in the maternity ward was a large room with a bed and a small cot, a wardrobe, and a TV screen with an attached bathroom.

Once Riona was settled, Danai left the couple inside and sat on the chair just outside the closed door. It was a flurry of activities with doctors and midwives coming and going. About an hour after they arrived, Riona was wheeled on a trolley to the birthing suite, where Danai and Zed were gowned.

She watched through the glass partition as the king's fourth grandchild was birthed.

It was the most surreal experience she'd had, witnessing another human make an entrance. It made her think of her mother, whom she hadn't spoken to in a while. The woman hadn't been part of Danai life for many years. After her parents' divorce, her mother remarried and moved to a different country. Danai hadn't seen her since she was in her late teens. The woman had a new family and other children. Danai thought maybe the woman didn't want her.

But having witnessed a live birth, she wondered how it was possible to give birth to another human being and not want them.

Danai had already accepted that she didn't want to have a child of her own. But she was no longer wary of other people's children. And she had Riona to thank.

She stayed with the princess when she returned to her suite in the maternity ward. The delivery had gone well, but she would be kept overnight.

It turned out that Danai needed this distraction. She hadn't thought about Prince Zawadi since their arrival at the hospital this morning, until visiting hour when the suite got busy with members of the Royal House visiting. Queen Zulekha was one of the first to come, accompanied by Prince Zareb and young Nour. Zawadi and Zik came afterwards.

Danai barely gave the crown prince a glance as she let them into the room but stayed outside.

Unfortunately, they all had to leave about an hour later when visiting time was over.

Danai checked the room. Princess Riona and the baby seemed to be taking a nap. She sat in the chair outside the door and closed her eyes. She could do with rest too. Yesterday's exhaustion was catching up to her. But coffee would have to do. There was a coffee machine at the end of the corridor.

A scuffing sound made her open her eyes. She gasped.

Prince Zawadi stood about a metre away. "Are you okay?"

Now that she looked at his face, there were worry lines and dark patches around his eyes as if he hadn't slept well recently. Had he been as restless as she had been. She doubted it. He had been adamant about rejecting her last night.

"I'm fine," she said. "Did you forget something?"

"No. I brought coffee for you." He held the polystyrene cup like an offering.

"Oh." She accepted it. He was back to being considerate. She'd confused it to mean that he felt affection for her. But she'd been wrong. "Thanks."

"You're welcome." He seemed hesitant to move. "Would you like to take a break?"

"I can't leave my post." She opened the cover of the coffee and stared at the black liquid before taking a sip.

"Amadu is by the nurses' desk. He can cover while I buy you lunch. I want to thank you for taking care of my niece and sister-in-law."

She shook her head. She would not let him trick her with his niceness. "It's not necessary. I was just doing my job."

"We both know it's not your job. Please let me buy you lunch."

She sighed. When he pleaded, she couldn't say no to him. "Fine. You can buy me lunch in the hospital cafeteria."

She wasn't even sure where else he'd wanted to take her.

"Great. Hold on." He walked down the corridor and came back a few minutes later with Amadu.

"Hi Amadu," Danai said. "Thanks for covering. The princess is asleep. Just listen out in case she wakes. Call me. I'll be in the cafeteria."

"No problem," Amadu said.

Zawadi and Danai walked down one floor to the restaurant. The place was almost empty. The lunch rush was over a few hours ago.

Danai ordered meat patties and fresh coffee. Zawadi ordered coffee.

They sat at a small round table. The server brought their order. She obviously recognised the prince by the way she fawned over him. To his credit, Zawadi was gracious.

When they were alone again, he waited for her to start eating before speaking.

"About yesterday. I messed up. I didn't tell you the whole reason for removing you from the rugby team, and the timing was wrong."

She drank some coffee to remove the food stuck in her throat. "What was the reason?"

"There was a complaint about you being on the team."

"From whom?"

"It doesn't matter. But it was someone I couldn't ignore."

Danai read between the lines. The only people he couldn't ignore around the palace were his parents. She nodded. "And the timing?"

"I should have waited a few days and allowed you time to enjoy the well-deserved victory celebrations. I'm sorry I ruined your day."

"I understand."

"About last night."

The pain of his words lanced through her as if she was reliving last night. "No need to rehash your words. You were very clear about your position." She shoved her plate aside and stood. "Let me walk you to the car, and then I'll send Amadu down."

He pursed his lips, nodded, and stood, looking disappointed.

But she would not be swayed. She'd practically bared her soul to him, and he'd rejected her. Last night was best kept dead and buried.

# Chapter Eighteen

*April 2020*

Zawadi averted his gaze from the shrub savanna vegetation whizzing past to Danai, who was in the front passenger seat. He sat at the back of the blacked-out SUV.

As usual, she wasn't talking to him. She hadn't said anything to him since the day in the hospital canteen after the arrival of Riona's and Zediah's newborn daughter. At least, nothing beyond the perfunctory greetings and necessities.

More to the point, he hadn't seen her smile or laugh. Not since the post-match victory celebrations. The same event he'd ruined by kicking her off the rugby team.

Somehow he knew kicking her off the team was the least of their problems.

She'd bared her soul to him, and he'd rejected her.

She had every reason to be furious with him. He'd been a jerk. It couldn't have been easy for her to tell him how she felt about him at the party.

Still, it seemed like whichever way he went, whichever decision he made, he was bound to get it wrong.

She—Danai—had ruined him.

As much as he'd yearned to accept the offer Danai had made at The Castle of 'one night only', he would have been unable to live with himself afterwards. He'd made an abstinence vow and a commitment to Amara. What kind of person would he be if he didn't honour the promise?

Yet now, he was miserable.

Miserable. A word he'd never associated with himself previously.

Until he could no longer have friendly banter with Danai every morning on the walk from his apartment to his office.

Turned out it didn't take her leaving the palace and never coming back for him to miss her. He missed her already, yet she was within touching distance in the same car as him, going to the same destination.

And to think there were other more pressing government matters than his relationship status.

Like putting the country under lockdown and restricting international travel for the citizens and foreigners as the COVID-19 pandemic spread through the globe and death tolls in Europe and Asia skyrocketed.

Companies were told to allow their employees to work from home where possible. Only essential services were allowed to go to work.

Because of the king's heart condition, the palace had to be quarantined, and everyone put into protective units. Unfortunately, many aspects of the virus were still unknown, and there was no cure or vaccine yet.

The government had to ensure the hospitals had personal protective equipment and oxygen tanks, which helped patients. So, they commissioned a factory to make face coverings and PPE.

A few weeks into the pandemic, the king and his consorts were relocated to Lake Miri palace, a smaller home, to help maintain the king's health.

Zik moved into The Castle with his staff. Zareb stayed in his house in Darusa city, while Zediah remained in DP with his young family.

Hence, Zawadi was in this car, in a three-vehicle motorcade heading to Somie, a rural commune in Northern Bagumi where his country home was located.

In less than two months, so much had changed in his life.

Actually, his world was turned upside down many months ago.

Nine months since he first met Danai when she and her colleagues captured Kweku and delivered him to Zawadi.

Six months since the assassination attempt on his life.

Four months since Danai showed up at the palace and became a part of his daily existence.

Sure, at first, he'd resisted her presence. Then he'd denied the attraction between them. Now, she'd relegated his position in her life to 'job' and had returned their connection to acquaintance mode. He hated it.

Hate. Another word he was unfamiliar with until recently.

For the first time in his life, resentment was like an unshakable shadow dogging his footsteps.

Zik. His mother. They'd been correct about his feelings for Danai. They'd formed a bond.

Danai was everything he shouldn't crave—a commoner, an employee, an unbeliever, and a woman who wanted to stay childless. She'd been quite adamant about it when he'd asked the question once.

Even if somehow, they surmounted all the previous obstacles. That last one would be impossible for him as the crown prince.

If Zawadi planned to become the future king, then his wife should give birth to the heir. He couldn't remain childless and become the king. The two were mutually exclusive according to the Bagumian constitution.

So, he shouldn't devote hours thinking about this. He'd been born and bred to be the future king of the nation.

And in about three months, he was set to marry Amara as his duty to the crown. To the future of Bagumi.

The sound of beeping horns announced their arrival at Somie. The cars went down the long drive set through acres of green lawn towards the three-storey modernised 19th-century country house. There were stables for the horses he owned and barns for equipment.

For the first time in weeks, happiness made his fingers tingle. Finally, he would get to ride his beloved horses. The more he thought about the animals, the more excited he became.

One of the first things he would do once he got out of the travel clothes would be riding.

Soon they were disembarking the cars on the circular driveway outside the house.

"Your Royal Highness, welcome home." The butler bowed deep along with the other masked servants, standing beside the portico.

Zawadi exited the vehicle, door held by Danai. "Thank you, Hakeem. Glad to see everyone looking well and socially distanced."

"Of course, My Prince. We all understand how important it is to follow the guidelines to keep our loved ones and colleagues safe."

The servants bustled and offloaded the luggage.

"Good." Zawadi smiled, happy the information drive seemed to be getting through to the population.

He walked through the open double front doors into the expansive foyer with polished stone flooring and cream walls. Sunlight coming through the high windows passed through the chandelier above his head and created prisms of colourful light across the room, turning it into an almost magical space. One of the reasons he loved this house, this space made him feel almost childlike and without worries.

His chest expanded as he sucked in a deep breath and let it out. Then he turned to Hakeem, who was slightly behind him on the right while Danai was on the left. "Hakeem, this is Ms Ruga. She is my new personal bodyguard. Please ensure she has everything she needs."

He didn't usually introduce his bodyguards. But Danai was more than a bodyguard, and he wanted the staff to give her preferential treatment. Also, she'd never been here before.

"Of course, Your Highness." Hakeem tilted his head and glanced at Danai. "Welcome to Somie, Ms Ruga."

"Thank you, Hakeem," Danai replied, her brown eyes shining with purpose above the black face covering. Dressed in her usual, her braids pulled into a ponytail and hands clasped in front of her.

"Hakeem," Zawadi spoke again. "I'd like to go horse-riding this evening before dinner. Please make the arrangements."

"As you wish, My Prince." The butler bowed again.

Zawadi headed up the grand curving stairway, Danai a couple of steps behind.

What was on her mind? He imagined her assessing all the possible things that could go wrong in this house and how to counter them. She was good at her job. He'd never had any reason to fault her.

At the top floor, which was his space in its entirety, he stood aside for Danai to do her checks.

She went from room to room. Other security men watched over the house even when he wasn't in residence. Preparations would have been made for his arrival.

As usual, she was thorough and took a few minutes to traverse all the areas of this level. She wouldn't trust someone else with the job that was hers to do. He knew this about her already.

"All clear, Your Highness," she announced, returning to the reception room.

"Thank you," he said and headed towards the master bedroom but paused as the servants turned up with the luggage. He changed direction and waved at the second bedroom on the floor. "Danai, this is your chamber. I hope you don't mind. I thought you'd like to stay close."

"Oh." She turned to meet his gaze, beautiful brown eyes searching, forehead furrowed. "Why am I here instead of the staff quarters?"

The urge to step close to her and brush the frown lines away from her forehead gripped him, and he shoved clenched hands into his pockets. "You are my quarantine buddy. So, we share the same space."

"Okay." She nodded, pain flickering in her expression as she broke eye contact.

A lump wedged in his throat.

"If you say A and you mean B, it's going to backfire," Zik's words came back to haunt him.

Zawadi wasn't wholly truthful. While they'd been in Darusa Palace, they hadn't shared the same quarters for quarantine. So, she could have a suite on a separate floor of this twelve-bedroom residence. But he didn't want her far from him. Seeing her often, even when she wasn't talking to him, was a consolation he wasn't willing to give up yet.

"Danai," he said and waited for her to look at him. "You can have a different room if you wish. But I would love your company on this floor. So…"

He trailed off as his stomach clenched and his heart raced. Would she choose to sleep elsewhere? He wouldn't blame her. After all, he wasn't offering anything more than companionship when she wanted so much more.

"No. This is fine." Her eyes sparkled with warmth.

His heart leapt. She was smiling for the first time in weeks. Shame he couldn't see the curve of her luscious lips.

"Thank you," he said and tugged his face covering off. "Since it's just the two of us here, we can do without these."

"Of course." She took hers off.

Sighing with pleasure at the friendly expression on her face, he swivelled towards his room. "I'm going to get changed. Then we can go riding."

"Eh." She cleared her throat. "Your Highness."

He glanced back. "It's Zawadi. Please."

She nodded, lips tugged up in a small smile. "Zawadi, is it okay if one of the other guards went with you?"

He faced her again, worry puckering his brows. "Why?"

She shifted from one foot to the other, looking uncomfortable. He'd never seen her look unsure. "I'm not very good with horses."

"Oh." He'd taken it for granted that she would be a horse-rider since she was so good at everything else. "You can't ride?"

She lifted one shoulder in a half-shrug. "I don't feel comfortable on horseback. I prefer machines to animals. If it were a motorbike or quadbike or even a mountain bike, I'd be there already."

"I see." There was nothing he could do for today. Most of the horses here needed competent riders. "Okay. Speak to Hakeem to assign someone else."

"Thank you, Your—" He raised his brow, and she changed it to "—Zawadi."

Smiling, he turned and entered the master bedroom.

***

"Tell me about this love you have for machines," Zawadi asked, weeks later at the dining table, Danai sitting across from him. The setting in here was more intimate than the formal banquet room downstairs.

They spent most of their time in this house aside from when he went horse-riding or walked with Danai. One evening because of a sudden downpour, they returned early from their walk. Danai caught a cleaner coming out of Zawadi's bedroom.

Although Zawadi had thought the woman had just cleaned the space, Danai had been suspicious and had gone searching. She'd found video-recording equipment stashed above the wardrobe, overlooking the bed. The woman had confessed as soon as Danai questioned her. Apparently, she'd been coerced by Nathan, whom she'd been having an affair with to spy on Zawadi.

Zawadi still hadn't recovered from the disappointment of finding out his assistant had thought he was having an affair with Danai and wanted to record it. Worse, the man had turned out to be the palace mole.

When Zareb arrested Nathan, the man threatened to spill Zawadi's secrets—about his alleged affair with Danai and his involvement with Kweku Doona's abduction from Cape Verde.

This, along with other issues were adding to Zawadi's stress level.

Each day was hectic, filled with video conferences with the ministers and dealing with new problems. Although the original lockdown had been for a few weeks, it had extended into three months. Students couldn't go to school. Adults had to work from home where possible.

Of course, not everyone was happy with the restriction, and protests had broken out in some places.

He checked in with his family in the evenings, ensuring everyone was well and telling them all to stay safe.

Because of the restrictions, the villagers could not work. Zik and Zawadi organised food banks and feeding drives to ensure those in remote locations were not adversely affected due to loss of income. His other brothers couldn't get involved. Zareb had his hands full, managing security at all the different residences with fewer available staff. Zediah had an infant daughter, Alayna, and a toddler son, Nour, keeping him busy.

So, Zawadi enjoyed sitting down to dinner with Danai. She was the only direct human contact he had daily. Hakeem only delivered the meals from the kitchen. And Zawadi was not in the same space when the cleaner showed up too.

Now, Danai looked at him, her amber eyes lighting up like it always did when she was excited about a topic. "Well, when I say machines, I mean automobiles, really. Cars and motorbikes mainly."

"Okay." Zawadi nodded in encouragement for her to keep talking. "Tell me about them."

"My father owns an auto shop in Bali. When I was a kid, I spent every day after school there. I would do my homework in the office, and afterwards, I could help with the cars. My parents divorced while I was young, so it was just dad and me. My uncle didn't like me being there. Didn't think girls should be working as mechanics. But my father didn't care. He taught me about engines. Taught me to drive. Even bought my first motorbike."

"You own a motorbike?" he asked, astounded.

"Yes. I'm on my third now. I prefer them to cars, although I appreciate the convenience and security of cars."

"I don't know much about bikes. But Zik is obsessed with race bikes and cars."

"Yes, I know. We've talked about it. He's offered to take me to an F1 Grand Prix race when things open up."

Her laughter tinkled, filling him with warmth. Yet his stomach clenched with jealousy because she had so much in common with his brother. Zik had already reassured that he had no interest in Danai. Still… "Are you thinking of taking him up on the offer?"

She shrugged. "It sounds interesting. But I would really rather play rugby."

"I've been thinking about that. How about setting up a women's rugby-sevens tournament? Same as we have the men's event. Would you be interested in leading the initiative?"

She lowered her cutlery on the plate and picked the glass of water. "So, I take it that I'm permanently off the Royal Princes' team."

He lowered his elbows to the table. "I know how I handled the situation was wrong. But the issues remain. Having you play in the men's game is dangerous." The image of the way Yusuf tackled her on the pitch made him clench his hands. "I just keep seeing that nasty tackle from Yusuf multiplied each time we play, and I don't want you to get seriously hurt."

Surprisingly, the warm sparkle returned to her eyes. "So, you kicked me off the team because you care about me. Not because of the archaic Morality and Decency laws."

She was teasing him. Winged creatures fluttered in his belly. There was nothing more beautiful to witness than Danai in good spirits.

"The archaic laws notwithstanding. Yes, I do care about you," he admitted, and the walls didn't collapse around him.

She beamed a full smile, lips tugged up gloriously. "Thank you."

He nodded, uncertain about what to do about the fuzzy sensation washing over him. Best to move along. He'd revealed too much. There was no point dwelling on feelings he could do nothing about. "I hope you will take me to meet your father one day. I want to meet the man who raised you."

"You want to meet my dad? Even though he's just a mechanic?" She looked flabbergasted.

"He's the human who raised you. Who made another wonderful human. I have total respect for such a person. And your love for him is obvious in the way you talk about him. It mirrors the way I feel about my father. Other people look at him and see a lofty king. To me, he is the man who raised me and loves me. I talk to him about everything. He is precious."

"That's the same thing about my dad. We can sit and talk for hours. His presence and his words soothe my worries."

Zawadi grinned. "Now, there's something we have in common. Our love for our fathers."

Perhaps it was time for him to speak to the king about Danai.

***

The trip to see his father didn't happen as soon as he'd wanted.

Zawadi and Zik met daily via video calls to discuss any issues. It was during one of those calls that Zik broke the news. One of their rugby teammates had caught the virus and passed on.

Zawadi was devastated.

His siblings were the closest people in his life. Yet, the rugby team was a family, and every member was more than a friend. Before the current restrictions, he'd met with most of them weekly and knew them as personally as it was possible to know others. They were his second family. So, he felt the loss as if it had been one of his siblings.

For days, he locked himself away, barely eating, avoiding conversations.

Danai kept the staff away from him as per his instructions. She was the only one allowed into his presence.

He cancelled meetings, even the regular ones he'd set up with family. Zik picked up his slack and took over the cabinet conferences in his absence.

Of course, his family didn't leave him alone. One day, Zareb showed up to check on him.

Between him and Zik and Danai, they convinced Zawadi to speak to a grief counsellor. Eventually, he did, and it took a few sessions before he began to articulate his emotions.

One evening, he sat with Danai in the small library. They usually retired here after their evening walks, before going to their separate beds.

As usual, he read a book. Sometimes she read a book, too. Tonight, she was drinking a glass of red wine. She wasn't on duty, so he had no problems with it. He just liked to have her company since they were quarantined together.

Tonight, he wished to discuss something with her, something life-changing but hadn't been sure how to broach it.

When Danai placed the wine glass aside and shifted to rise from the settee, Zawadi stopped caring about rules and protocols.

He tilted his head and raised his hand, cupping her cheek. It was the first time he'd touched her intentionally. He, who wasn't tactile, who eschewed romantic gestures, was attempting to be romantic.

Her skin was smooth milk chocolate. Her breath hitched, seemingly from shock by his action. Her lips parted slightly as if an invitation to kiss her.

The big moment didn't pass him by—the seriousness and consequences of his actions, not just on his life but on the kingdom.

He, who had never deviated from the plan set about when he was born, was about to take a massive detour.

He hesitated, teetering over the edge of an invisible cliff. This oasis was far removed from the rest of the world. Yet, others would feel the impact of his deeds.

For months they'd lived in this desert palace, where he was surrounded by vaults of ancient scrolls and shelves of books. He'd immersed himself in his favourite pastime—studying and preserving his country's history and culture.

Yet, he'd discovered something else. A yearning so intense, so overwhelming, he was coming undone at the seams.

Danai, on her part, stayed composed. Aside from the steady pulse at the base of her throat, she didn't show any anxiety or annoyance. Instead, her brown eyes seemed to watch him without judgement, which strengthened his resolve.

She understood the risk he was about to take, had never pressured him into doing anything about the spark that existed between them. The time they'd spent together, her always by his side—the conversations they'd had. Slowly, over time, without knowing it, he'd become emotionally attached to her.

Then she'd laid her cards on the table, told him she cared about him. She'd seen his vulnerability, his fears, and hadn't been repulsed. Hadn't thought less of him.

Now she waited, perhaps wondering if he would take this to the next level and kiss her.

He wouldn't get physical with her, not without severing his connection to the woman he was betrothed.

But first, he had to lay his cards on the table. He had to be truthful to the woman who had come to mean the world to him. She'd been here, beside him as he'd gone through the worst phase of his life.

"Danai," he said, his throat thick. "A few months ago, at The Castle, I wasn't frank with you. You were correct. There is something between us. Something beautiful. Something I've never felt for anyone else. Something I want to keep for the rest of my life." He swallowed. "I know that I'm asking for a lot, especially after what I did to you. But please give me another chance."

"What are you saying?" she sounded breathless, just like he did.

"I'm saying that I want you. Not just for sex. Not just for today. I want you for the rest of my life. I'm in love with you."

"Oh, Lord. Are you serious?" Her eyes shone brightly.

"As serious as I would ever be about anything."

"But you're engaged."

"I know. I will end it today. Just tell me you feel the same, my love. Tell me you'll stand by me no matter what happens."

"Oh, Lord. My stomach is flipping." She clutched her midriff. "My heart feels like it will punch a hole in my chest."

"I feel the exact same way." He took her soft hand and placed it over his thumping heart. "Please, my love, tell me you feel the same because I'm about to give up everything for you."

"But I don't want you to give up everything," she protested, and he loved her more for it.

"The choice is to stay as the crown prince or be with you. I choose you. I love you."

"Then, yes. I will stand by you. I love you too."

He leaned forward and pressed his lips against her. His life was about to go from non-stop meetings to zero. An empty calendar. He didn't care as long as he had this woman beside him.

He leaned back and looked her in the eyes. "Do you think you could live with me forever?"

"Well, I've lived with you for the past three months, and we haven't killed each other. So, I think we'll survive forever." She winked at him.

And he could only agree.

# CHAPTER NINETEEN

*July 2020*

"You look beautiful," Zawadi whispered in Danai's ear as the car pulled up outside Lake Miri, his father's countryside residence.

They were in the back seat of a car together for the first time since she'd met him.

Zawadi had made peace with his feelings for her and was taking her to meet his parents. She was going to meet the king in a few minutes as Zawadi's partner.

She swallowed the apprehension knotting her stomach.

Someone opened Zawadi's door, and he stepped out into the bright sunlight. Another liveried valet opened her door, but Danai waited. She had practised getting out of the vehicle with Zawadi as they'd done with other protocols.

Now she was his partner. She had to adhere to some royal etiquettes, like wearing a maxi dress and covering her head for formal meetings with the king.

Two weeks ago, Zawadi had declared his love for her, and they'd become a couple, unofficially.

Due to the restrictions, he hadn't seen his parents to tell them in person, and he didn't want to do it over the phone.

So, they'd waited until a partial restriction had been implemented, allowing people to see their loved ones. But no large gatherings were permitted yet.

Two days ago, they'd gone to Bali, and Zawadi had met her father. Oumou's mother had made a fuss over him, excited that one of their children was settling down.

Now, Zawadi came around and extended his hand to help her out. He was regal and gorgeous in the ceremonial flowing purple tunic and trouser set, feet in leather loafers.

Taking the offered arm, she swung her legs onto the stone-paved courtyard and straightened. The beautiful teal tulle dress skimmed her curves and cascaded to her ankles strapped in black leather heels. Her hair was styled in a chignon, and she wore makeup—all styled by Oumou. Her stepsister had turned up in Somie yesterday laden with all the beautiful things Danai wore today. Her sister-friend was always showing up for her.

Danai hoped the royal family would be impressed because she looked like a fairy-tale princess. At least, she felt like one.

Zawadi's eyes had widened in awe when he'd seen her all dressed up. Then again, he was a man in love. He wouldn't care if she was dressed in rags. Or so she hoped.

Still, Zawadi nan Ibrahim Saene, crown prince of the kingdom of Bagumi, was in love with her, a girl from a small town who liked to get greasy under vehicles or sweaty on a rugby pitch.

The thought made her lips curl into a smile as they walked up the short stairs and through the front door, hand in hand. Another surprise since he wasn't the most tactile man in the world.

As they walked deeper into the magnificent house, which was almost as grand as Darusa Palace, her apprehension returned. She remembered her first meeting with Queen Zulekha months ago. Zawadi's mother had been unimpressed then. Was this such a good idea? Her hands shook.

"Relax." He flexed his fingers through hers as they stopped outside the door she assumed led into the king's reception room. "No matter what happens in there, I'm with you."

She glanced at him and allowed her face to relax. "I know."

They'd talked about all the possible outcomes of this get-together. She would admit that for the first time in her adult life, she was petrified for him. The future was unknown to them.

With the palace mole apprehended, she was no longer needed as Zawadi's bodyguard and was awaiting reassignment. However, she didn't know how her bosses would take the announcement of her involvement with Zawadi. She could lose her job since going undercover would become impossible as the crown prince's spouse.

And for him, the likelihood of losing his position as the future king was high.

The uniformed guard opened the door and announced them. "Your Majesty, presenting His Royal Highness, Crown Prince Zawadi and Ms Ruga."

Zawadi squeezed her hand and released it before stepping into the chamber. No public displays of affection were allowed in the king's presence, so they couldn't hold hands in there.

Danai followed, keeping pace beside him as they walked along the short aisle. Low padded armchairs lined the walls of the spacious throne room, along with ornaments and high ceilings.

On the dais directly ahead was the king on the ornate throne, dressed in white and purple ceremonial robes and turban. The veiled queens sat in gilded padded armchairs to his left, while Prince Zik sat in an armchair to his right.

She stopped when Zawadi stopped. He lowered his body, prostrating and touching his father's velvet-slipper, while she knelt.

"Long live His Majesty," they chorused.

"Zawadi," his father's voice boomed cheerily. "It is wonderful to see you in Lake Miri after so long. How are you, my son?"

"I'm well, Papa." Zawadi straightened but didn't approach to embrace his father. They were social distancing for the sake of the older people. They'd been tested to ensure they were virus-free before making this trip. "You look well too."

"I feel well, thank you."

"Mama, Mum, you both look great too." Zawadi genuflected.

"Thank you," Queen Zulekha said, although her expression was unreadable.

"You're welcome," Queen Sapphire smiled.

"Good to see you too, Zik," Zawadi greeted.

"Good to see you too, bro. Danai." Zik's smirk said he had sussed the situation.

"Go ahead and introduce your guest," Queen Zulekha sounded impatient.

"Papa, my mothers, I wish to present my love, the woman I will spend the rest of my life with, Danai Ruga."

Queen Sapphire gasped.

Queen Zulekha's face hardened. "So, you decided to take a second wife, after all. I told you I could have smoothed this out months ago. Does Amara know about this already?"

Danai touched her stomach, hoping to settle it.

Everyone seemed to be staring at her, well, at her and Zawadi. The king's expression was unreadable. Queen Sapphire looked shocked. Queen Zulekha looked annoyed.

"No, mother," Zawadi said, glancing at Danai with a smile. "I'm not taking a second wife. Danai will be my only wife when she finally agrees to marry me."

Danai had initially dismissed his marriage proposal because she'd wanted to be sure about the outcome of this meeting. They were still navigating things, like his devotion to his Faith, which she couldn't deny him. He was happy to accept her. But what about his family?

"What?" Zawadi's mother expression darkened.

"My son," the king spoke quietly. "Do you understand the consequence of that statement?"

"Yes, Papa. I understand that by not marrying Amara Onoh, I'm giving up my rights to the throne. It was not an easy decision for me to make.

All my life, I have been prepared for the throne. I've spent the time doing what everyone expects me to do but not what I want to do. Until Danai came along. For the first time in my life, I feel like I'm finally living on my own terms."

"You can still have it all," Queen Zulekha interjected. "Just keep to the marriage contract with Amara Onoh. As I said, I'll make her understand. You can marry both. Or does your new *love* not understand our traditions?"

She seemed to spit the word 'love' out with contempt which wound Danai up.

She stiffened. She might not be royalty, but she didn't deserve to be spoken to in that manner. "Your Majesty, I understand some of our traditions are old-fashioned and need updating. I love your son and will stand by his decisions. However, I will not share his bed with another woman."

"I agree with Danai," Zawadi said. "We are content with each other. She is the only woman for me. I pray for your blessing, Papa."

His father sighed and nodded. "You have it, my son. I wish you and your chosen the joys of a happy union."

Dear reader, thank you for reading The Tainted Prince.

For the first time, I wrote an entire romance novel without a smidgen of a love scene. I feel I should explain why. And it's simple. Zawadi, and to an extent Danai, just didn't go there. He was not that kind of character. He didn't let me into his sexual thoughts. So, it's not that he doesn't have them. He just didn't show me.

I know you've come to expect sex scenes from my stories. But I can only go where the characters take me.

So, I hope you understand. Zawadi and Danai will be back later, in a Royal House of Saene holiday special. Hopefully, they'll let us into the bedroom then.

On a sexy note, I should say that Zik more than makes up for Zawadi's restraint in his story, The Future King. He even has a dungeon in The Castle!

And I'm sure you would have already guessed that Zik's love interest is Amara. So sexy shenanigans will be plenty. I promise.

In the meantime, please leave a review of The Tainted Prince and let me know what you think.

The Future King is coming in February 2022. It's available to preorder now.


Keep reading for teasers from the next 2 books in the Royal House of Saene series, **The Future King by Kiru Taye** and **The Illegitimate Prince by Empi Baryeh.**

# ROYAL HOUSE OF SAENE

## THE PRINCESSES:

His Defiant Princess by Nana Prah

His Inherited Princess by Empi Baryeh

His Captive Princess by Kiru Taye


## THE PRINCES:

The Torn Prince by Zee Monodee

The Resolute Prince by Nana Prah

The Tainted Prince by Kiru Taye

The Illegitimate Prince by Empi Baryeh

The Future King by Kiru Taye

## Excerpt from THE FUTURE KING (Royal House of Saene #8) by Kiru Taye

"What have I done to you to deserve this hatred?" Zik asked. He understood her anger, considering the circumstances. However, he was the good guy here. He'd done the decent thing.

Still, the level of vitriol in her tone indicated there was more going on.

"You're not Zawadi," Amara bit out in a contempt-filled voice, her gaze fixed at a point beyond his right shoulder, her chin tilted imperiously.

Zik staggered backwards. That fucking hurt. He hated being compared to his older brother. He'd done everything not to be like the 'perfect' Zawadi. However, it seemed he'd fallen way short of Amara's standards.

"And yet he jilted you." As soon as he said it, he regretted it. She was hitting below the belt. Didn't mean he had to hit back.

Her eyes widened and then narrowed. The haughty expression returned to her face as she straightened her shoulders. "And that shows how low I've fallen when I end up with a jerk like you."

"Excuse you." Zik stalked towards her. "Zawadi jilts you, and *I'm* the jerk? Just in case it skipped your mind. I saved your face out there. I stepped in and rescued you and your family from the public humiliation."

The palace press coordinator spun the story in the media—Zik and Amara had always been in love. Zawadi's abdication only provided an opening for them to be together.

"Exactly." She glared at him, not budging when he stopped an arm's length away. "It is your brother's mess, and you're the one cleaning it up. So, you will put up with my scorn and hatred for however long I deem it reasonable."

## Chapter One from THE ILLEGITIMATE PRINCE (Royal House of Saene #7) by Empi Baryeh

*New Year's Eve.*
*8 months earlier ...*
"You should have been a prince."
Kalahari 'Kal' Asanti stilled at the words—words so similar to those his mother had uttered on several occasions; words he'd learnt at an early age to dismiss as the romanticism of a woman who, despite the hand life had dealt her, had still believed in fairy tales. Unfortunately for his Mamaa, she didn't get the happily-ever-after she'd never stopped believing in. Even on her death bed when the irrefutable truth had laid bare the lie she'd stubbornly clung to all these years, she'd played her final card and revealed a secret she should have taken to her grave.

The truth had unleashed venom into Kal's heart and set him on a path of vengeance. Instead of the tearful reunion she'd hoped for, his mother had ensured the downfall of the man she claimed to love.

She had one thing right, though. He was indeed going to meet the Saene family of the kingdom of Bagumi—the first step in his plan to destroy the man he should have called father. King Ibrahim Aziz Saene.

Soft footsteps behind reminded him he wasn't alone. The Zanzibar Convention Centre brimmed with thousands of guests attending the annual Children's Foundation Gala, one of the biggest charity events in Africa. Tickets were pegged at a thousand US dollars each, with the proceeds going to several charities across the continent. Like most such events, however, many attendees used it for networking, some to brag about their altruistic deeds, and others for the opportunity to rub shoulders with the rich and mighty.

Normally, he avoided such pomp and pageantry. The way he saw it, there had to be something fundamentally wrong with making a big show of one's good deeds. He preferred to make anonymous donations to many of the causes he supported. He'd broken protocol this time for one reason only:

To observe the enemy.

As luck would have it, King Ibrahim was the guest of honour this year, a privilege which came with the price tag of a hefty 'donation'—a gimmick undoubtedly meant to garner some international media attention. An hour into the event, neither the king nor a representative had made an appearance. His absence hadn't slowed down the festivities, though.

Finding the glitz and glamour strenuous, Kal had stolen out of the massive ballroom and taken refuge on one of several balconies. As it turned out, his escape from the flashlights and idle conversation hadn't gone unnoticed.

He gritted his teeth, bringing his mind back to the present and the person who'd interrupted his solitude. The last thing he needed was the company of a stargazing woman who'd spent a thousand dollars in hopes of catching the eye of a prince. Someone ought to save her from herself and rip the plaster off that fantasy. He was as good a candidate as any. After all, he might be the son of a king, but he wasn't Prince Charming. The sooner he made that clear and got rid of her, the better.

"What makes you think I'm not royalty?" He turned, lips pursed to dish out some tough love, yet the words didn't form.

He found himself entranced by the way the lights from the ballroom played against every rounded curve, awakening something primitive in him. She looked to be about five-foot-six, discounting the extra height afforded by her shoes. Her face remained shrouded in the dimness of the balcony.

Intrigued, he knew he'd pay any price to find out what she looked like. She stepped forward, and suddenly, her face was bathed in a beam of light slicing through the darkness from ... he didn't care to check where.

She held him captive with the most exquisite eyes he'd ever seen. An intense brown, like smoked honey, with a sparkle of gold in the left one where the light reflected off it. Their radiance would have laid his soul bare if he hadn't been standing in the shadows. With her entire face concealed behind an elaborate tattoo of ethnic make-up designed to give the appearance of a veil, she was mystery personified. She made easy prey of him as desire flared in his being with a fierceness that challenged reason.

Her effect didn't end at the physical, though. It ran deeper, reached him on an instinctive and spiritual level. Like a soul mate.

He shook away the errant thought, hoping she hadn't sensed his momentary confusion.

"For one," she started, "you're hiding out here instead of basking in the limelight."

He quirked a brow. Hiding?

Her lush lips curved up, revealing an even row of pearly whites invoking a vision of her nibbling on his earlobe. Somehow, he knew her teeth on his skin would be—

He snapped out of the reverie, forcing his mind to focus. Clearly, his unintended celibacy—the result of focusing too intently on revenge—needed to be rectified. How long had it been? Six months? More?

She mocked him with a chuckle. "I saw you inside. You were the picture of boredom."

Now he realised it wasn't her first remark that had snagged his attention, but rather her voice. It had an ethereal quality that seeped through him and did the impossible. He'd always felt restless, had often grappled with a compulsion to move, to do, to be on alert. When she'd spoken, the ever-present static in his mind had quietened. Her voice had stilled the storm within him. The sudden calm slammed into him with such force, he nearly doubled over at the impact.

By God. What was this?

He took in a deep breath, quelling the mêlée of shock and euphoria, told himself this couldn't possibly be real. Perhaps his thoughts of vengeance had tripped his senses, lured him into a trap of his own emotions. He never relied on sentiment to make decisions in any facet of his life—especially when it came to bedding a woman.

Whoa! When did he decide he was going to sleep with her?

He ignored the taunt, having no time for misgivings. He never hesitated when going for something he wanted, be it a company or a woman.

She hadn't taken another step forward, as if intentionally putting herself on display for his pleasure. His gaze snagged on her elaborate 'veil.' Masks were popular at the gala. She hadn't gone for the norm, though, something she could simply take off. The tribal undertones made it even more arresting, made her more captivating. A jewel hiding in plain sight.

Who was this vision in a piece of elegance and with the delicately cupped breasts that would fit perfectly in his hands? His eyes narrowed, lingering. No. They'd spill over just enough to entice his lips to them. Her waist, covered entirely with layers of stringed gemstones, tempted him to glide his hand over them. Would she feel the warmth of his touch?

He balled his hands into fists of resistance.

While he enjoyed the visual excursion she presented, he'd much rather she were displayed for his viewing in full naked glory, so he could adore her curves as they were clearly meant to be. What would she do if he held her? What if, emboldened, he pulled her forward, captured her full lower lip in his teeth, and nibbled? Would she offer him her tongue? Wrap her arms around him? Invite him to discover the treasures concealed beneath her clothes?

Merde! He reminded himself of the futility of his imaginings. Her first statement had made it clear she sought a prince. Bile rose his throat—a testament to the extent of his distaste for the notion.

"I'm not a prince, and I don't desire to be one. You might want to move along."

She raised a hand and fluttered her fingers in a queenlike fashion. The title of queen would certainly suit her. She possessed the looks, the grace and … that extra something many women searched for but most never found.

"If I were looking for a prince, I'd be inside," she said. "I came out here to find you."

A giddy sensation exploded within him, chasing away the darkness engulfing him at the idea of her and Prince Charming together. However, a sliver of suspicion rooted him to the ground.

As a man on a mission that could bring down an entire nation, he couldn't take anything for granted. He'd been discreet in his reconnaissance of King Ibrahim and the Kingdom of Bagumi. As a successful financier specialising in corporate takeovers, discretion counted for everything. He'd taken all necessary precautions, but now, he wondered if he'd allowed his hatred for the man to affect his focus. Had he failed to cover his tracks as well as he'd thought?

He needed to distract her. Experience told him of one sure way to achieve it. Seduction.

He stepped out of the shadows, stopping close enough that he could reach out and touch her.

Satisfaction brewed and swelled as he noted her sharp intake of breath.

"You look far too innocent to utter such words."

Her gaze dropped, colliding with his chest. Her lips parted as her focus hastened back up. Instead of the apprehension he'd expected, desire stared back at him. His pulse responded with exuberance. For the first time tonight, he began to see the bare-chested warrior costume his stylist had foisted on him as a plus.

She blinked, visibly regaining composure. "I didn't know innocence could be judged by sight."

Sassy. He'd give her that.

"There's a lot I can discern at a glance."

"You sound confident."

"I have no reason not to be."

"Maybe innocence is part of my act."

He searched her eyes. They were open, guileless—like someone who had nothing to hide.

He shook his head in absolute conviction. "Except it's not. I see it in your face, your expression ... your persona. You couldn't fake it if you wanted to."

The moment he finished speaking, the desire which had been receding surged back into her eyes and socked him in the chest. It revealed exactly what context she'd taken his words. In seconds, his mind went right there with her.

"Would it bother you?" she asked in a soft, almost hesitant voice.

"Innocence is a quality easily affected by many women." He paused, unable to prevent his gaze from roving over her as less-than-virtuous thoughts saturated his mind. "The true kind is refreshing."

"Now I'm sure you're no prince. Their education doesn't include flattery."

He caught a whiff of her scent—something wild yet feminine. It taunted every masculine cell in his body, but he didn't want to scare her with his considerably bigger stature. He held her gaze.

"I don't flatter, Honey Eyes. I may flirt with danger occasionally, tempt fate even, but flattery isn't in my nature."

"Danger?" She laughed, an incredibly beautiful sound, ensnaring him like a siren's song. "Do I look dangerous?"

"Said the splinter to the lion. I'd tread carefully if I were you."

"If I'm the splinter, then perhaps it's you who should be careful."

He allowed a smile. "I consider myself forewarned."

Their gazes locked. Heat flared between them. This time when she blinked, she couldn't sweep away her desire. Flirting had brought them to a crossroads. Turn right to keep going; left to retreat. He waited for her to make the call, half-expecting her to take Door Number Two—seek refuge in more innocent banter or invent an excuse to return to the party. Safety in numbers and all.

"I've been treading carefully my whole life," she surprised him by saying. "Tonight, I walk on the wild side."

He laughed softly. Maybe not so innocent, after all.

"The wild side, hm? I can take you there, my splinter, if that's what you want."

By now, he was certain she had no link to King Ibrahim. His intelligence team would already have alerted him. If word had somehow reached the king of Bagumi about Kal's investigations, it would seem he'd picked the one person alive who could momentarily shift his focus.

"Take me there, Warrior." Her sweet command, though whispered, drowned out every other sound.

He extended a hand. "Come."

She stared at his proffered invitation, indecision warring with desire in her eyes. Their relative sizes occurred to him anew. At six-three, he towered over her by nearly a foot. His muscular build and warrior costume—though overly embellished—probably didn't help. The arm guard with metallic tentacles snaking up to form a cuff around his biceps, already a snug fit, suddenly seemed to be cutting off his blood supply. A faux leopard skin cape draped over his other arm provided the only covering for his upper body. Even the shendyt covering his loins didn't make him look any less ... manly, as his brother had put it.

Then again, she'd been the one to encroach on his privacy. She didn't get to look at him as if he were a menace. He posed no threat. Unless she turned out to have an agenda. In which case, she— and whoever had sent her—would discover the most dangerous predators struck without warning and inflicted deadly bites.

He vacated the thought, preferring to return to the exhilaration of bantering with her.

"You hesitate."

She snapped her head up, her eyes colliding with his. For the briefest of seconds, he witnessed a depth of desire he hadn't expected without having even touched her yet. He saw something else. Lust. Pure and unbridled, as if it had been brewed in the cauldrons of Eros.

"It isn't hesitation if I already know what I want."

She placed her hand in his. The contact, a spark of electricity, compelled his fingers to close around her hand instead of the instinct to pull away as if from danger. Yielding to the force which had led them to this point, he tugged her into his arms, draping her left arm over his shoulder.

As her supple curves melded against him, she tilted her head fully in a natural motion to meet his gaze. Her lips parted as though she'd resorted to breathing out of her mouth. They beckoned, but he resisted the urge to dip his head for a taste, knowing the build-up of anticipation would make the eventual surrender more satisfying. If it didn't kill him first.

"Dance with me," he said.

He swayed her sideways, the beginning of a waltz. The crystal beads surrounding her waist rubbed against his lower abdomen, causing erotic friction. If he didn't start a conversation to get his mind off how good it felt, he'd be hoisting her on his shoulder and hauling her off to the nearest bed.

"What do I call you?" he asked.

"No names," she whispered in a tone laced with urgency.

He raised a brow, curiosity aroused, then tempered it down, deciding against probing.

"Too bad. My name would sound beautiful on your lips."

No matter how much she affected him, this would unfortunately be a one-time deal. After tonight, he'd be embarking on a dangerous mission, one which couldn't accommodate the entanglements of a woman awaiting his return.

Yet, it didn't keep him from wondering at her reasons for wanting to hide her identity. Who was this woman, and why did he want to unravel her secrets?

## OTHER BOOKS BY LOVE AFRICA PRESS

Love on a Mission by Jomi Oyel

Note Worthy by Dhasi Mwale

Forever and a Day by O.L. Obonna

Saving Her Guard by Kiru Taye

## CONNECT WITH US

Facebook.com/LoveAfricaPress

Twitter.com/LoveAfricaPress

Instagram.com/LoveAfricaPress

www.loveafricapress.com